THE JAPANESE PRINCESS

China, 1927. Communists and Nationalists are fighting each other and bandits and warlords plague the country. Imperial Japan is eager to provoke a war and when Princess Sadie, a member of the Japanese Royal Family, is kidnapped, her life is at stake as her death will be the excuse for Japan to invade. The mission of Common Smith V.C. and the crew of the *Swordfish* is to rescue Princess Sadie before she loses her life. It is a race against time – and if they don't succeed, the terrible consequences could well bring about the start of World War II.

THE JAPANESE PRINCESS

THE JAPANESE PRINCESS

by

Charles Whiting

Magna Large Print Books
Long Preston, North Yorkshire,
BD23 4ND, England.

British Library Cataloguing in Publication Data.

Whiting, Charles
   The Japanese princess.

LINCOLNSHIRE
COUNTY COUNCIL

A catalogue record of this book is
available from the British Library

ISBN 0-7505-1907-X

First published in Great Britain 1996
by Severn House Publishers Ltd.

Copyright © 1996 Charles Whiting

Cover illustration © G.B. Print

All rights reserved. The moral rights of the author to be identified as author of this work has been asserted by him in accordance with the Copyright, Designs and Patents Act, 1988

Published in Large Print 2003 by arrangement with
Eskdale Publishing

All Rights reserved. No part of this publication may be reproduced, stored in a retrieval system, or transmitted in any form or by any means, electronic, mechanical, photocopying, recording or otherwise without the prior permission of the Copyright owner.

Magna Large Print is an imprint of Library Magna Books Ltd.

Printed and bound in Great Britain by
T.J. (International) Ltd., Cornwall, PL28 8RW

Author's Note

Captain Sir de Vere Smith, V.C., or 'Common Smith, V.C.'* as he was known to the popular press in the '20s, had been fighting that strange 'war in the shadows' for nearly ten years when he and the loyal crew of the *Swordfish* vanished from Europe in 1927.

Ever since Smith had won 'the secret V.C.', as the press named it, he had carried out some perilous and vital missions for British Intelligence. But in 1927 when Smith and his crew set out to cross half the world to get to China, little did they know that this was to be the most vital mission of all. For not only were they to prevent a war between Japanese Imperialists and Chinese Nationalists,

*In 1918 when de Vere Smith, the second son of the Earl of Beverly, was recovering from the wounds which he suffered while winning his V.C. he was asked by a woman journalist whether his name was spelled 'Smythe' or in any other form due to his aristocratic background. He replied he was just 'Common Smith'. The name stuck.

but also to ensure that the British Empire in the Far East didn't collapse due to that war.

In a China swarming with soldiers, bandits, traitors and whores, with its ancient customs and where 'foreign devils' could disappear easily without trace, they fought a strange complex, undercover action, not only against Japanese Imperialists, Chinese Nationalists and Chinese Communists, but against the great River Yangze itself.

In his diary for 30 September, 1927, Common Smith recorded: 'Left China this day. Glad. The country is too cruel, complex for me. Death comes too easy here.' Nearly seven decades later it seems that little has changed.

C. W. York, 1995

PREFACE

To Steal A Japanese Princess

'You speekee da English?' the fat perspiring man from the *Tribune* asked hopefully.

She simpered, giggled, hiding her white-painted face, slashed with scarlet lips and wriggled in apparent nervousness as she knew all Occidentals expected Japanese women to act, and hushed, 'Yes, I speak.'

'Swell,' the fat man from the *Tribune* said in relief, eyeing the girl's figure which even her too bright kimono couldn't quite hide. 'Say, then I can ask you a few questions, yeah.'

She fluttered the ivory fan in front of her beautiful face, again as if she were very nervous.

'I speak very slow,' the correspondent said, mouthing the words in an exaggerated fashion. 'You understand then. You answer. Okay?'

'Okay,' she answered, wondering if she should say 'very good'. But she decided she wouldn't; that would be overdoing it.

Behind the fat American, the traffic and life of the Bund flowed back and forth. Rickshaw men, skinny but with legs like athletes; old crones with big straw hats, hobbling by on their deformed feet, shouting their wares, important Europeans in their big cars, with their Chinese drivers hooting their way through the throng, great bearded Sikhs in turbans, dark eyes full of suspicion, ready to wield their bamboo staves at the slightest provocation. All was noise, smell, heat and dust. She told herself she had not seen anything like it in Japan, even in Tokyo. No wonder they said that Shanghai never slept.

'You come to Shanghai to marry General Kameyama,' the American said. 'Why you marry General? He very old. Maybe three times older than you.' The sweat poured down his pudgy face as he posed the laborious questions, as if he were talking to some idiot child.

Behind her Taisho, her bodyguard, frowned, his face set and hard under his shaven skull. Only peasants should sweat. Educated people should never sweat. It meant a loss of 'face'.

'I ordered to,' she answered, simpering once more, waiting to spring her surprise on this impudent American. 'By Emperor.' She drew in her breath sharply, as a sign of respect. Behind her Taisho did the same, though he didn't understand a single word of English.

'Wow,' the correspondent exclaimed, scribbling hastily on his pad, the beads of sweat dropping onto it from his forehead. 'By the Emperor himself. But gee, how can Emperor Hirohito order you to marry, if you don't want to...' He realised suddenly that she might not have understood and repeated himself. 'Why Emperor make you marry, eh?'

She looked at him. Now that Japanese simpering look had vanished to be replaced by one of aristocratic disdain. 'Because,' she said firmly, 'I am the property of the Emperor – as is the whole of Japan. I do whatever the Emperor wishes.'

The correspondent looked at her in sudden amazement. 'Say,' he exclaimed, 'you speak good American!' He pushed the sweat-stained Panama hat to the back of his balding head, as if he couldn't quite believe his own ears.

'So I should,' she answered in perfect English, savouring his astonishment and discomfort a little, wondering at the same time where the car was that the General had promised to send to pick her up on the Bund, once her ship had docked. 'My late father spent a small fortune to send me to Smith five years ago.'

The man from the *Tribune* whistled softly through his teeth. 'An ivy league college. Not many Japs – er Japanese,' he corrected himself, 'go to those kind of schools.'

She didn't respond so he said. 'You said the Emperor owns you. How come?'

'The Emperor owns the whole of Japan and its people,' she said.

'Holy cow!' the man from the *Tribune* said.

Inwardly she smiled. She had her own private thoughts about the Emperor, but she was intent on putting down this fat American, who had appeared totally out of the blue and had begun asking personal questions. 'The Emperor is a god,' she went on. 'Doctors are not allowed to touch the imperial body unless they wear silk gloves. His tailors must never touch him. They must measure him up from a distance. When he travels through the streets, no one must look down upon the Imperial person. Every window shade must be drawn too. Traffic police must commit hari-kari if they misdirect the Emperor's car. Train drivers must do the same if they arrive more than a minute late with the Imperial person on board...'

She reeled off the details, knowing that some were lies, enjoying the look of growing awe on the American's face as he scribbled them down, repeating to himself as if it were a litany, 'you don't say ... well dogone, you don't say...'

She kept him scribbling a little while longer. Then she got bored. She turned to Taisho and snapped, 'Where is the General's car? It should have been here by now.'

Taisho, who had been a sergeant in the General's regiment once, bowed swiftly and said, 'Yes, Princess. There is something–' He stopped short. Abruptly his hand reached into his right pocket where he kept his pistol. Too late!

The knife sliced through the air. It caught him in the centre of his chest. His mouth dropped open suddenly. He fought to keep on his feet. To no avail. His knees began to crumple beneath him.

Her delicate hand flew to her mouth in fear. 'Taisho!' she cried.

'*No, not me*,' the American's shriek ended in a sudden gurgling noise. She swung round again, as Taisho died at her feet.

A husky Chinese, who had been lounging against the wall opposite a moment before, eyes half-closed and face too calm, as if he might have been drugged on opium as most of the workers were, had darted forward with lightning speed. In his big hands he had a garrotting rope. Deftly he threw the one end around the fat American's neck and tugged hard. Now the man from the *Tribune* was struggling furiously. His eyes were bulging from his head like those of a man demented. His face was puce and strange. Terrible strangling noises were coming from his gaping mouth, as he clawed at the killing rope, in vain.

'What the Sam Hill is going on?' she demanded, too startled to know it was no use to ask in English.

Up at the street corner the big Sikh policeman started to shrill furiously at his whistle, as more and more Chinese 'workers' began to crowd around the Princess and the dying American. A European car skidded to a stop. An elderly man poked his head out of the window and yelled, 'What the bloody hell do you Chinks think you're ab–' A Chinese hit him with a wooden club. He reeled backwards into his seat, blood jetting in a scarlet arc from his split skull.

Princess Sadako, 'Sadie', as she had been known to her sorority sisters at Smith, was a quick thinker. She knew she was in trouble.

This had all been staged to get at her. The 'man from the *Tribune*' had probably been 'greased' to hold her up with questions like this, while whatever had been planned was sprung upon her. Hurriedly she reached into her ornate, bejewelled handbag. There she kept the pistol her dead father had given her when she had been sent to the States. He had been afraid she might be attacked by gangsters like those they showed in the Hollywood films.

As the fat American died, kneeling at her feet, tongue hanging horribly out of his mouth like a piece of purple leather, she clicked off the safety catch.

Too late!

A pock-faced Chinese, still wearing the pigtail which had been banned years before, pushed his way through the crowd of assailants. She pointed her pistol at him, knowing that he presented the greatest danger. He knocked it to one side with his hand. Her shot flew wildly into the air. With his other hand, he thrust a pack of wadding at her face. He grinned evilly at her, as she choked at the acrid smell.

He grabbed her with his free hand. She struggled wildly. In vain. The Chinese with the pigtail had the strength of an ox. The pistol tumbled from her suddenly nerveless fingers. Her legs began to weaken. There was a great roaring in her ears. The chloroform was having its effect. Her last memory before passing out was that of her assailant's hand groping between her legs and that of the man chuckling with delight as he did so. Then she felt herself being lifted. A black mist fell before her eyes and she knew no more...

A hundred metres away, General Kameyama let the curtain of the big De Soto fall back in place. 'They have taken her,' he said solemnly to his companion, Captain of Intelligence Moto. 'You have done well, Moto.'

Moto, plump, bespectacled, undersized, allowed himself a brief, gold-toothed smile. He drew in his breath as a sign of respect in the manner which Army Regulations prescribed and said, 'Thank you, General.'

The General didn't seem to hear. He hunched there over his samurai sword, his breath rasping through his ruined lungs, the only sound in the back of the big American car from which they had watched the kidnapping of the Princess. His ancient wrinkled face, covered in liver spots, looked worried. Moto thought he knew why. The General knew he had committed a grave crime. He had had his own bride-to-be kidnapped. Moreover Princess Sadako was a relative of the Empress, a member of one of the five most aristocratic families in Japan. If anything went wrong with the great scheme, Moto knew that the General would be forced to commit hari-kari. He too, probably.

Outside on the Bund, the sirens of police cars hurrying up to the scene of the kidnapping shrieked. Police shrilled on their whistles and bellowed threats at the Chinese. A stone rattled against the side of the American car.

The sound roused General Kameyama from his reveries. With the ivory hilt of his sword, he tapped the blacked-out window which separated them from the driver.

'*Hi*,' the driver barked and started the big car.

Moto looked out of the corner of his eye at the General's ancient face. The worried look had vanished. It had been replaced by a look of steely determination: that same determination that had made him a hero of the war against the Russians over twenty years before. 'It must be done,' he said through lips which seemed to be worked by tight steel springs, 'for the sake of Nippon and our beloved Emperor.' He drew his breath in sharply and bowed in the direction of Tokyo.

'For the sake of Nippon and our beloved Emperor,' Moto echoed the words reverently.

Slowly the wheels of the De Soto crunched over the bodies of the fat American and Taisho. Their blood mingled with the sprig of cherry blossom the Princess had been planning to give to the General. Then they were gone...

PART ONE

The Heathen Lot

Chapter One

C looked ill. The once square, hard face had hollowed out and become flabby. The hand the two young men shook as they entered his rooftop office in Queen Anne's Gate was no longer as hard as the teak, which he had once scrubbed as a young midshipman in the Navy. It was weak and without energy.

A little wearily he returned to his seat behind the big desk which had once reputedly belonged to Nelson. He let the two ex-naval officers wait. So they pondered why he had summoned them here to this strange house, the headquarters of the British Secret Service, with its hidden staircases and disguised lifts and tough bronzed officers who looked as if they might kill you for sovereign and who had probably done just that.

With a sigh, C adjusted his monocle and stared at the two of them – Smith, V.C. known throughout the United Kingdom as 'Common Smith V.C.', and his second-in-command 'Dickie' Bird. He liked the cut of their jibs. Again he told himself the two young men represented the best Old England had to offer. As long as the public schools kept producing such men, brave, resourceful, patriotic, the King-Emperor had nothing to fear as far as his Empire was concerned.

'You're going to China.' C broke the heavy silence of that strange office, littered with maps, aeroplane models and rows of bottles and test-tubes which suggested chemical experiments.

Smith whistled softly.

Next to him Dickie Bird said in that slightly dotty fashion that he favoured, though he had already won the DSO at the age of seventeen in the last war, 'Gosh, that's a bit much isn't it. China, what ho!'

C gave him one of those look with which he had frightened many an officer when he had been on the quarterdeck of the dreadnought he had commanded before the war. 'Yes, you are to take one of those new flying boats out to Shanghai. Should take you about a week to get there.'

De Vere Smith's lean handsome face hardened. He felt his heart beat more quickly. They had been on the beach in East Yorkshire for nearly three months now with little to do and he and the crew of the *Swordfish* were getting bored. Besides, the men were missing the special allowance which they received when they were on ops. 'Do you mean there's a show, sir?' he asked quickly.

'Yes,' C replied, 'and a damned unholy mess it is, too.' He frowned at the window. The spring rain was striking the panes with bitter hard slashes. The raindrops ran down them like cold tears. 'Perhaps you saw that cartoon in last week's *Punch?* It seemed to me to sum up the confused state out there. China's in absolute anarchy.'

'Yessir, I saw it,' Dickie Bird replied in that purposelessly mindless voice of his, 'British Tommy guarding the wire at the International settlement at Shanghai and a lot of Chink laundrymen waving their fists at him and the Tommy's saying, "Now then, move on Mr Chu Chin Chow. I don't care which side you be on, but if you be going to kick up a row, you must keep outside. Inside here's private property."' He beamed winningly at the Secret Service chief.

C pulled a face and looked hard at an unabashed Dickie Bird. 'Yes,' he said, 'but it's worse than just the attacks on the foreign international settlements in Shanghai. The place, that is the whole of China, is in such a state of turmoil that it is not only our business interests which are threatened. At the moment the whole of that part of Asia could erupt into war – something which the Empire can simply not allow when we're having trouble enough in Egypt and India, not to mention damned Ireland.' He sighed like a man sorely tried.

'*A war*, sir!' Smith exclaimed. 'I know that the Chinese Nationalists have been having a go at the Chinese Communists, but that's been going on for quite a while now. But a real all-out war–' He broke off a little helplessly.

C nodded at him slowly. 'You heard me correctly, Smith, an all-out war in China, involving ourselves, the Japs, probably the Reds,' he meant the Russians, 'and even those spineless creatures, the Americans, who seem to be totally dedicated these days to letting other people pluck the hot chestnuts out of the fire for them. It would be an absolute catastrophe!'

'I see, sir,' Smith said slowly, though he didn't. Still he wondered what role he and the crew of the *Swordfish* could play in what was to come. In the past C had sent them out on a good few important missions, but nothing of this kind. He waited impatiently for C to explain what their mission was to be.

But C took his time. Perhaps, Smith told himself, the head of the British Secret Service was quite ill. Usually he kept his statements short and sweet, often to the point of bluntness, even rudeness. 'I don't think,' he said slowly, staring out at the cold rain, 'I have ever faced a situation like this since the war.' He frowned again. 'It's all so confusing. One wonders where really to start.'

Dickie Bird flashed Smith an enquiring look. Smith shrugged slightly, as if to indicate that he couldn't do much about C's new indecisiveness.

'As you know,' C continued slowly, even painfully, 'an armed struggle is going on in that far country between the Chinese Communists under a peasant leader named Mao Zedong. We know little about him save that he is absolutely ruthless. He is opposed by the official leader of China, the Nationalist leader, General Chiang-Kai-Shek. We know more about him, but he is, too, absolutely ruthless. Both of these leaders hate the foreigners who live and trade in the International Settlements in their country, British, American, French, Japanese and the like. We have, as you both know, our own police, troops and administrations out there, running the Settlements as if they weren't on Chinese soil. Naturally the Chinese dislike that.'

Dickie Bird pouted his lips contemptuously. 'Damned impertinent devils,' he snorted. 'Those Chinks don't know what's good for them.'

'Well said, Bird,' C agreed with a show of heartiness. 'But it's typical, you know. So few of those we rule in the British Empire, blacks, browns, yellows, realise just what a privilege it is to be governed by the King-Emperor. But back to our problem. Other forces are at work out there as well as the two warring parties of Chinese. The Japs are intent on extending their empire at the expense of the Chinese if they can do it. They are just waiting for China to fall apart so that they can move in. Then there are the Reds. As always they are intent on disrupting the democratic world when and wherever they can—'

'So it's somewhat of a four-sided affair,' Smith interrupted a little impatiently, hoping to speed things up. 'Chinese Nationalists, Chinese Communists, the Japs and of course, the Russians.'

'Exactly, my boy. Now something has happened, which may trip off an international incident, the spark that could possibly ignite the timber as it were.'

Smith swallowed hard. Obviously this why C had summoned them to London from Yorkshire. 'What is it, sir?' he demanded without any attempt to hide his eagerness.

But C did not answer immediately. Instead he said, 'I think I'll leave the explanation of that to an old friend of yours.' Before the two young men could react, C pressed the bell on his desk in front of him.

Outside the red light, which indicated that C was occupied, changed to green. The door was opened almost immediately.

'*McIntyre!*' both Smith and Bird exclaimed, as they rose to their feet to greet the newcomer. '*Captain McIntyre!*'

'*Major* McIntyre,' said the tough Canadian Intelligence Officer with the ribbon of the Military Cross on the breast of his tunic and with the bulge in his pocket which indicated that, contrary to regulations, he was still carrying a revolver. But, as Smith told himself, the big 'Colonial' with the crooked grin on his ugly face, had never been one for regulations.

Hastily the three of them shook hands and Smith noted automatically that McIntyre had lost the pallor he had had when they had last seen him in Germany four years before. Indeed he looked quite bronzed as if he had been in the sun a great deal.

McIntyre saluted awkwardly and then without waiting to be asked, tossed his cap at the hat stand and sat down. 'The Huns ran me out of Germany last year,' he said, talking as always out of the side of his mouth, eyes restless, darting back and forth, as if suspecting there might be trouble at any moment. 'Place simply got too hot for me. So now I'm back with the "Hell's Last Issue", the Highland Light Infantry to you – *officially*.' He pulled a crumpled green packet of *Woodbines* out of his pocket, lit a cigarette with a match and dropped it onto C's carpet.

'Unofficially,' C said, apparently not angered by McIntyre's dropping of the match on his precious Persian carpet, 'the Major works undercover for me, and only a few of our own political police out there know what his real job is.'

'Which is,' McIntyre said, breathing out twin curls of smoke slowly, 'keeping tabs on Commies, Chink crooks and the general run of cheap rats in Shanghai. And believe you me, there's more than plenty of them.'

He sucked hard at his cheap cigarette once more.

McIntyre, Smith told himself, was running true to form. Like most 'Colonials' he was not awed by authority, as the British mostly were. He knew the type. Thousands of McIntyre's fellow countrymen had volunteered to fight for the 'mother country' in the last show. Coming over as private soldiers, they had fought in those terrible battles of 1916 and 1917 – and those who had survived the great slaughter had been commissioned in the field to become temporary 'officers and gentlemen'. Not that McIntyre would ever be mistaken for a gentleman. He was too angry, tough-looking and outspoken for that. All the same, Smith knew, the hulking Canadian was a good man to have at your side in a scrap. He had had ample proof of that in the past.

'Now then,' C resumed, 'I've had McIntyre flown specially back to London to brief you. He will fly back with you to Shanghai–'

'What about the *Swordfish?*' Dickie Bird interrupted urgently.

C understood the two officers' concern about the former naval torpedo boat which had served them so well over the last years when they had undertaken so many secret missions for Britain. 'There's no time for the *Swordfish*, Bird,' he said. 'However the China Station chaps are going to place one of their most modern craft at the disposal of you and your crew. It was built at the Thorneycroft yard last year. They tell me it's a really fine top league craft.'

'Spiffing, sir,' Dickie Bird chortled, happy at the news.

McIntyre nearly swallowed his cigarette at the word 'spiffing'. But he contained himself. He knew the languid, weedy ex-naval officer, with the receding chin, was not the cream-puff he looked – by any means.

'All right, McIntyre, pray tell Smith and Bird here what you've already found out,' C said and sank back into his chair a little wearily, as if everything was an effort for him these days.

McIntyre stabbed out his cigarette on the heel of his boot, took a look at the rain still slashing the window angrily and said, 'It's not that much. But here goes. First of all, I'll say this.' His hard blue eyes flashed from one face to the other, as if he were challenging them to question him. 'A Jap princess who was to marry the Jap general commanding their settlement in Shanghai has been kidnapped. It's going to be our job to find her. Because if we don't, it might well just be the incident,' he paused momentarily to let his words sink in, 'that'll start World War II. Now this is how it began for me and my assistant, Mr Chen...'

Common Smith V.C. was not an imaginative man by any means. Now, however, he was no longer listening to the tough Canadian. For his thoughts were elsewhere, as a cold finger of fear traced its way down his spine. *'God no,'* a faint hushed voice whispered at the back of his mind, *'not another world war...'*

Chapter Two

Carefully the two men crept down the quay. It was shrouded with wet fog. Out in the harbour the ships were sounding their fog-horns. Muted and sad-sounding they were the only sounds which disturbed the melancholy stillness of the night.

Up ahead a yellow light appeared. It marked, McIntyre knew, for he had come this way earlier that day, one of the Japanese control points: a little wooden sentry box raised slightly above the ground, from which the sentry could control the entrance and exit of the barefoot coolies who worked on the docks.

'Mr Chen,' he whispered to his interpreter, 'we'll go round the back of it. If the sentry makes any trouble, no weapons. Use your blackjack.'

Mr Chen, who boasted he had gone to Oxford after service in France with a Chinese Labour Battalion (something which McIntyre didn't think true, though the tubby little Chinese certainly spoke several languages including French, English and Japanese fluently) smiled blandly.

'Will be done, Major,' he whispered back in the same formal manner that the Canadian used with him. They had worked together for a year now and both respected the others' abilities and talents. Their relationship was now that of comrades working together rather than that of master and employee.

They had been following Captain Moto, the Japanese Intelligence officer, ever since Mr Chen had heard the rumour that he was meeting with the *hunhulze*, the 'red beards', as he called the Shanghai river pirates. 'Is it possible, Major,' Chen had said in that strange oblique manner of his, so that a statement of fact was always turned into a question, 'that Captain Moto would meet with the red beards?'

McIntyre had nodded his agreement. It was very strange indeed, especially as the Japanese were committed, as were the other international authorities at Shanghai, to destroying the river pirates who terrorized the shipping trade along the Yangtze River.

Now reacting to a tip-off given to Mr Chen by one of his numerous contacts in Shanghai's thriving underworld, they were following Moto to a new rendezvous with the 'red beards'.

Hardly daring to breathe, the two of them started to cross behind the sentry box. McIntyre knew exactly what would happen to them if they were discovered. The Japs would cut their throats, weight their bodies and drop them into the muddy river. If they were ever discovered, the river pirates would be blamed. That would be that.

They came level with the little structure. No sound came from it. No light. Not even the smell of an illegal cigarette. McIntyre looked at Chen in the pale yellow light and nodded. Chen nodded back. They had done it. Moments later they disappeared into the shadows, where the big Canadian halted out of earshot of the sentry and started to screw a silencer on his automatic. 'Never can tell, Mr Chen,' he whispered.

'Could the Major be possibly expecting trouble?'

'No, Mr Chen,' McIntyre answered amused, in spite of the tension of the moment, at the way Chen always spoke. 'But as the ruddy boy scouts say – always be prepared. Come on.'

They penetrated deeper into the fog, the only sound the mournful howling of the ships' foghorns. Next to the quay now, there were the rows of anchored sampans, bobbing up and down on the slight swell, but absolutely silent. McIntyre told himself that the Chinks in those frail craft were born, lived and died on them without ever setting a single foot on land. Funny lot. But a dangerous lot as well. Most of the Chinks were honest enough, selling their wares to the big steamers and cruise liners coming in from Japan and the States. But a sizeable minority belonged to Mr Chen's 'redbeards', effectively hidden in this floating world, where it was virtually impossible for the police to control them, men – and women, too – who would sell their own mother for a handful of yen.

Pistol loose in the pocket of his raincoat, both men sticking close to the shadows cast by the dripping walls, heading for the place where Mr Chen's spies told him the Jap and the 'redbeards' would meet. 'It's the sewers which lead off from the Bund, don't you think?' Mr Chen, who of course already knew the location of the meeting, had said. 'Moto, you can say, eh, can approach that way unseen. It is possible that the 'red beards' will similarly be hidden in their approach from the water?'

Now the two of them approached the head of the inspection tunnel which led to the sewers below. Almost immediately they were assailed by the awful stench. Hurriedly McIntyre clamped his lips closed. He told himself he'd puke if he breathed in any more of that stink. Mr Chen appeared unmoved. But then, McIntyre told himself, the whole of China stank to high heaven.

On tiptoe they started to descend into the inky gloom. Rats scurried away from them in the darkness. They could hear their clawed feet running down the tunnel. Mr Chen switched on his torch carefully. The walls leapt into view, dripping stench and slime, the outlines of the fleeing rats magnified in grotesque, gigantic distortion. McIntyre told himself he wouldn't like to get trapped in this hell hole.

They turned a bend. Hastily Mr Chen caught his arm and held him back. Wordlessly he nodded to the hole just in front of McIntyre. A newly sharpened bamboo stake was propped up inside it. 'A trap perhaps?' he whispered.

'Too bloody right a trap,' the Canadian agreed with feeling. One step more and he would have surely been impaled on the stake. It was clear they weren't on a wild-goose chase. There was someone down here all right and they were taking precautions. A few moments later, McIntyre's suspicions were confirmed. Amid the stench of the sewers, he could smell the highly perfumed smoke of the kind of cigarettes the Japanese preferred. Captain Moto, or one of his representatives, was down there all right. He clicked off the safety catch of his automatic. Behind, Mr Chen did the same.

They pushed on.

Now they could see the yellow light streaming from the tunnel and hear the muted sound of several voices speaking. Mr

Chen cocked his ear to one side and listened intently before saying, 'Japanese perhaps, Major?'

McIntyre gave him a tight grin. 'Then the Jap is down here all right. But what the Sam Hill has he got to do with the river bandits?'

Mr Chen shrugged. Hurriedly he clicked off the torch and they stumbled forward, feeling their way by means of the dripping stinking wall, the voices getting louder all the time.

They halted at the bend in the sewer, the noxious fluid lapping around their ankles, wreathing them to the knees in the stinking steam that came from it. Cautiously, very cautiously, McIntyre peered round the edge of the wall. It was Captain Moto all right, outlined in the yellow glare of a ship's lantern which one of the 'redbeards' held. He was talking fast to a great ruffian of a Chinese, with a patch over his right eye-socket, in Japanese, while the rest listened, occasionally asking what the little Japanese officer was saying.

McIntyre pulled back and whispered in Mr Chen's ear, 'What do you make of it, Mr Chen?'

Chen shook his head for him to be quiet and listened more intently before whispering, 'Perhaps redbeards are accepting Jap money for help to Jap officer.'

'What kind of help?' McIntyre demanded.

Mr Chen cocked his head to one side and listened even more intently, as the filthy waste lapped around their ankles, the liquid agitated by the waves of a passing steamer further out in the river.

'Kidnap,' Mr Chen said laconically after a moment. 'Redbeards appear to be asked to kidnap – for money.'

'Kidnap who?' McIntyre rasped impatiently. At that moment a big black rat sprang from the water and bit the Chinese with the eye patch. He let out a great yell of surprise and fear, for even the river pirates knew that these black rats spread the dreaded plague.

The redbeard pushed Captain Moto aside roughly and, pulling out the pistol from the sash around his waist, began to fire wildly at the rat swimming away in the noxious sludge. His followers surged forward, slashing at the water with their curved swords, suddenly carried away with the thrill of the chase, while Captain Moto looked after them as if they had suddenly gone mad.

McIntyre realised their danger at once. 'Come on Mr Chen,' he hissed. 'Let's beat it. They're coming this way.'

As imperturbable as ever, Mr Chen replied, 'It appears that way, Major.'

The Chinese with the eye patch swung round the corner. He spotted them immediately. The rat was forgotten at once. He skidded to a stop. Next instant he yelled something in Chinese. McIntyre and Chen didn't wait to find out what it was.

Splashing and stumbling they waded their way through the slime as fast as they could. Slugs howled off the walls. The darkness was split by scarlet stabs of flame. The noise was ear-splitting. Once McIntyre paused for a split second. He turned and fired without aiming. A shrill scream rang out, echoing and re-echoing in the stone channel. There was a splash. Someone had fallen into the mire. Then the big Canadian was running once more.

They came to the tunnel through which they had entered the sewers. McIntyre pushed Mr Chen through. He turned and even as he did so, he knew that his action would alert the Japanese sentry on the quayside. But there was no other way. He pulled the pin from the little Mills bomb and tossed it in the direction of their pursuers and then he was running after Mr Chen for all he was worth.

'Mr Chen shot the Jap. Clean through the heart,' the big Canadian announced, staring hard at his three listeners, while the cold rain beat at the windows with increased fury, as if determined to break the glass. 'Then we scarpered. Next morning, so Mr Chen's informers told him, Captain Moto, the Jap Intelligence Officer, had vanished. At least no one has seen him at Jap HQ since that night in the sewers.' He lapsed into silence, taking out another of his cheap cigarettes, lighting it up and staring moodily at the rain, as if he had a lot of things on his mind.

In the end it was C who broke the heavy brooding silence with, 'There are still certain areas of this business which are unclear, gentlemen, but this much is certain. A marriage had been arranged with the Japanese general commanding at Shanghai. His bride-to-be, Princess Sadako, has been kidnapped by these river pirates and somehow this Jap secret service wallah Moto has a hand in the game. What exactly, we don't know at the moment. But what we *do* know is that Tokyo is threatening all sort of dire reprisals against China if the princess is not returned speedily.'

'Oh my sainted aunt!' Dickie Bird exclaimed in his dizziest manner. 'It's *cherchez la femme* sort of thing, what.'

C silenced him with a hard look. 'The Nationalist government has promised to do all it can to have her returned safely,' C continued. 'So far there's nothing from the Communist. Naturally they're happy to see the Nationalists in a fix–'

'But the funniest thing of all,' McIntyre interrupted, stubbing out his *Woodbine* almost angrily, 'General frigging Kameyama, the bridegroom-to-be, is doing sweet Fanny Adams to find his betrothed. *Now what do you make of that, gents?*'

Chapter Three

'Yer Chinkees are a heathen lot, ye ken,' CPO Ferguson intoned, as the big flying boat started to slow, the pilot feathering his engines noisily, 'but they're a canny lot.'

'Oh ay,' Ginger Kerrigan said without too much interest. 'You been here to Shanghai before, Chiefie?' The red-headed Liverpudlian winked at his oppo, fat-bellied Billy

Bennett. 'Come here with Nelson did yer Chiefie?'

Chief Petty Officer Ferguson glared at the young sailor, but didn't vent his usual rage whenever his age was mentioned. It had been a tiring seven-day journey, from Southampton, via Gibraltar, Alexandria and then on to Bombay and Hong Kong, and he wasn't in the mood. 'Ay I've been to the South China Station before,' he agreed, 'before the war. That's when I got to know the Chinkees.'

'Is it true, Chiefie, that the slit here goes a different way than with our women?' Billy Bennett asked in his amiable slow manner.

Ferguson ignored the remark and, pointing through the port hole, said, 'D'ye see that junk over there, with yon birds on the bow?'

The other two bent and followed the direction of his gaze. The harbour was crowded with ships of all nationalities, but there were plenty of Chinese craft as well – sampans, junks, yuloks. 'Yer, I see the birds, Chiefie,' Ginger Kerrigan said.

'Well them's cormorants. The Chinkees train 'em to eat fish when they're young and then when they're older they make 'em catch fish for 'em.'

'Go on,' Ginger Kerrigan said scornfully, tugging at his long nose. 'Birds won't fish for 'umans, even if they are Chinks.'

'They do,' Ferguson said stoutly. 'Look at yon bird.'

One of the cormorants had risen into the warm blue sky, trailing a rope attached to its neck behind it. Suddenly it fell out of the sky, plunged into the water and came up a moment later swallowing a large fish.

'Now watch,' Ferguson snapped, his faded old eyes excited under his grizzled thatch of cropped hair. 'Now ye'll see what I'm about.'

Lazily the bird flew back to the junk, still trailing the rope behind it to where a barefoot coolie was waiting for it. He acted immediately. As soon as the big bird had landed, he grasped the rope with both hands and tugged hard. The bird wriggled desperately and flapped its wings. To no avail. Its beak was forced open and out popped a large fish, flopping up and down on the deck in silver fear. The coolie let go of the rope. He stepped over to the fish and gave it a mighty blow across the head with his club. It was dead immediately and he tossed it into the already half-filled basket.

'Well I've seen every frigging thing,'

Ginger Kerrigan gasped. 'No fish and chips for me, Chiefie, not while we're here in Chinkland at least.'

Up front Smith grinned and, with McIntyre and Dickie Bird, he took in the sights of the port which bustled with all kinds of activity, with small boats coming and going all the time, while on the docks, bare-legged rickshaw boys raced to and fro, carrying self-important Europeans to their businesses, dodging in and out of the hordes of pedlars and beggars, all crying and shouting at the same time.

'Richest port in the whole of Asia,' McIntyre said, as the flying boat finally came to rest and the four engines were switched off. 'That's why we want to hang onto Shanghai and why the Chinks and Japs want to take it over. Rich pickings. Look over there, for instance. That's another Chink war junk. In the last few months there's been more and more of them sailing up the Yangtze from the Chink northern capital at Nanking.'

A gaily painted junk with paper sails and powered by hand-driven paddles was proceeding through the muddy water, past the gleaming white destroyers of the Royal Navy, all polished brass and scrubbed decks.

'But I say, old bean,' Dickie Bird objected.

'Can't see a damn gun on her.'

McIntyre gave his usual tight brittle laugh. 'They don't have any. They try to get as close as possible and then the crew throw stink bombs at the enemy vessel.'

Smith returned McIntyre's hard little smile and said, 'Well, that's the kind of enemy I like to face up to. I can stand the stink. At least it can't kill you.'

'You can say that again, old chap–' Dickie Bird began and then stopped short.

An immaculate white steam pinnace was heading for the flying boat with an officer in starched whites, complete with polished brass telescope, on its deck. 'The welcome committee, I suppose.'

'Yes,' McIntyre agreed. 'He's from the RAY.'

'The what? Who's that when he's at home?' Bird asked.

'Rear Admiral Yangze,' McIntyre answered.

'Gosh,' Smith said. 'Do you mean we've got a rear admiral commanding a river?'

McIntyre nodded. 'Yes, you know the Yangtze and all its adjunct waterways is as big as Western Europe.'

'I wasn't too good at geography at Dartmouth,' Smith said apologetically. 'But an admiral commanding a river!' He shook his head in mock wonder.

The rating on the bow of the pinnace positioned his boat hook against the hull of the flying boat so that the craft would not bump against the plane, while the officer in the starched whites sprang the intervening gap with his telescope still clasped beneath his arm.

He blinked at the sudden darkness of the cabin after the brilliant sunshine outside and said, as he stared around at the crew of the *Swordfish*, all dressed in rough civilian clothes, 'Glad to see you're in civvies. Spies everywhere nowadays in Shanghai. Mr Smith?'

'Over here.'

The flag lieutenant touched his hand to his cap in salute and said, although he was senior in rank and age to Smith, 'Glad to meet you in person, sir. Heard a lot about you – and – er Victoria Cross.'

Smith felt himself blushing. Dickie Bird giggled. The Lieutenant looked surprised.

'Okay,' McIntyre snapped, his mouth moving as if it were worked by tight steel springs. 'What's the deal?' He looked up hard and tense at the officer.

'Rear Admiral Yangtze presents his compliments, sir,' he said after a moment. 'He asks you if you'll have the flying boat to the end of the Bund where the insects are anchored.'

'Insects?' McIntyre queried sharply.

The Flag Lieutenant smiled. 'That's what we call the class – our gunboats. They're all named after an insect – *Butterfly*, *Moth* and the like – so we call them the insects.'

McIntyre grunted something and then got up to pass on the order to the pilots.

Ten minutes later they were seated under the immaculate white awning which covered the forward six-inch gun of HMS *Glowworm*, a heavily armoured gunboat which lay low in the water, facing the RAY.

Admiral Crutch, known behind his back in the Yangtze flotilla as 'crotch', was one of those no-nonsense old seadogs, who had seen and done everything, and who spoke in a loud voice as if he were bellowing in a Force 10 gale, his sentences articulated in short chopped-off fragments. 'Sun not over yardarm yet... Still think this calls for a pink gin.' He clapped his big hands and a Chinese steward appeared from nowhere, tray with bottles and glasses at the ready.

Silently he flitted from guest to guest pouring the drinks and then when he was

THE YANGTZE RIVER, 1927

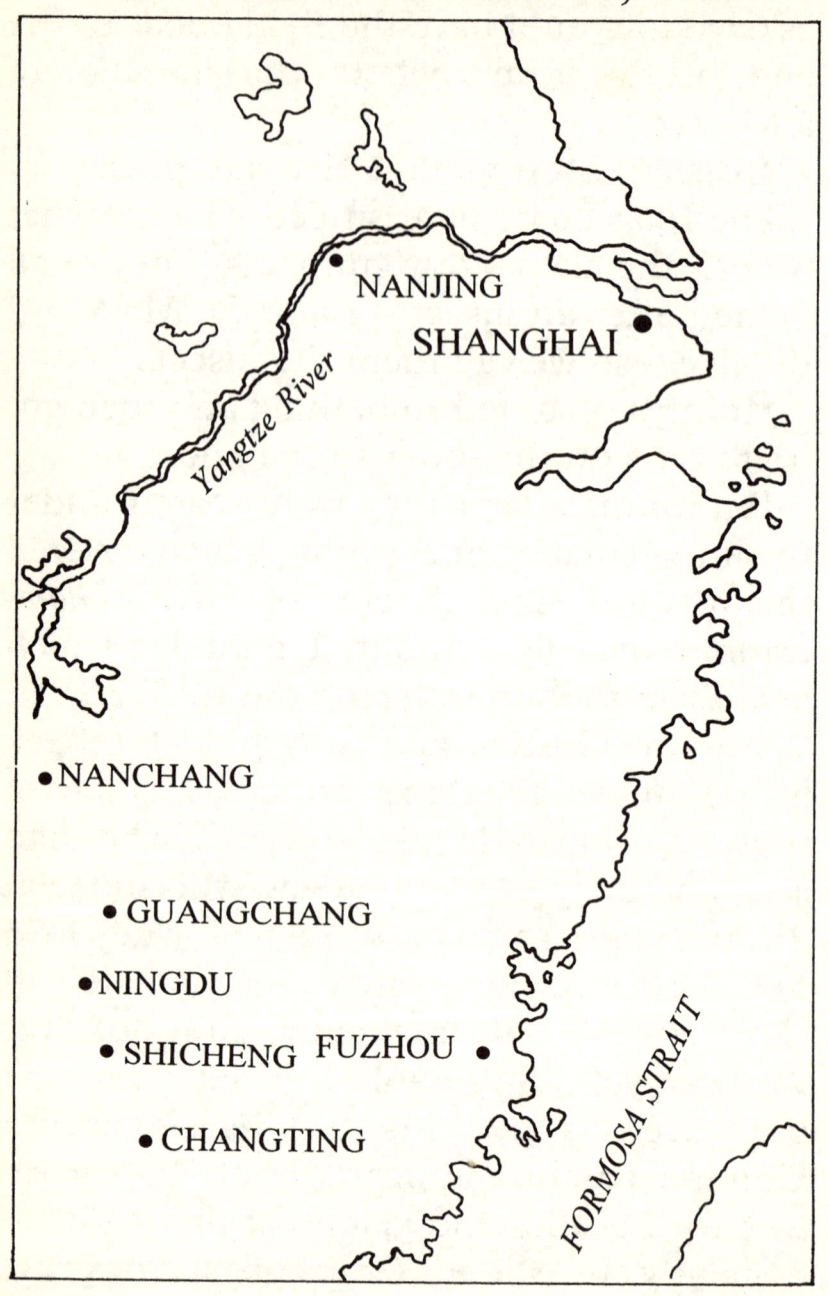

gone, the Admiral raised his glass in toast. 'Chin-chin,' he barked. 'Better times would have asked have you brought your polo sticks. Sporting pieces, too. Get some good shooting out here, you know. Snipe to wild boar. Not now.' He took a hearty swig of his drink, coughed and frowned. 'Japs and Chinks getting restive. All the Jap Navy ships have been taking on ammo and supplies. The Chinks are telling their people here to strike. Probably Communist agitators behind that one. And we've had several incidents of the usual "foreign devil" stuff. You know throwing stones at our chaps and the like. Situation boiling up to a head, what.' He frowned again, looked at the bottom of his glass, as if he were disappointed at what he saw there. Then he drained the rest of the contents. 'Cut a long story short. Come on over to the chart here, gentlemen,' he barked and rising to his feet walked over to the map of China pinned to the side of the gleaming six-pounder. Obediently they followed.

The Admiral cleared his throat. 'Here we are at the mouth of the river. I've got two gunboats here – at Shanghai. The rest of a flotilla of eleven are stretched out along the Yangtze as far as east of Nanking. Our job is to protect British traffic between there and here from Chink Pirates and the like.' He grunted and glared at them, as if challenging them to say something. None of them, including the tough Canadian dared, so he continued.

'Now here at the Upper River,' he pointed to a spot some hundred miles from Shanghai, 'I've got the *Cockchafer* stationed.' Again the Admiral glared at them, as if daring anyone to make a comment about the gunboat's name.

Again his listeners were silent, for even Dickie Bird dared not be flippant about it.

'Linking the *Cockchafer* with my flotilla to west and east, I've got one of the latest Thorneycroft pinnaces. Beautiful little craft. Fast, tough, armed with a quick firer and a twin Lewis gun. She's yours, my boy,' the Admiral said to Smith, 'for the rest of this nasty business.' He forced a wintry smile. 'And I want her back in good shape when you've finished with her.'

Smith returned his smile. 'Do my best, sir,' he said. 'But how are we going to get to the – er *Cockchafer*, sir?'

The Admiral turned to McIntyre. 'This Chink chap of yours – Chen. He's hired a junk to take you there. 'Fraid I can't spare a craft. Remember though the old pirate trick, Major. A couple of 'em hire on as deckhands. When their dirty thieving pals attack, they head for the bridge and stop the ship.'

Inwardly McIntyre wondered what Mr Chen would have made of being called a 'Chink'. He always referred to his compatriots, as 'Chinese gentlemen', just as he called the Britons, 'Honourable British gentlemen'. Out loud he said, 'Mr Chen's a shrewd old bird, sir. He'll have taken care of that.'

'Hope so.' The Admiral turned to Smith once more. 'When can you get underway, Smith?'

'Give me tonight, sir. My chaps have been cooped up in that flying boat for seven solid days. They deserve a chance to stretch their legs.'

The Admiral smiled. 'Wine, women and song, eh? But not too much of the women, Smith. I'm told they've got some very peculiar diseases out here. All hearsay of course.' Then he winked solemnly at the young officer. 'Just hearsay.' They were dismissed...

Chapter Four

'Now pin back yer lugs and get this,' CPO Ferguson growled grimly, as he and the rest of the *Swordfish* crew pushed their way through the crowd of sailors from every nationality at the entrance to the brothel. 'Shanghai Lil's a respectable knocking shop. So behave yersens. I'll gi'e ye an hour – and that's that. Use one of them french letter things and wash yer John Thomas careful afterwards.' He eyed the excited young sailors coldly. 'I'm not having any of my men coming down with one o' them filthy diseases.'

Ginger Kerrigan winked at Billy Bennett. 'Christ, Chiefie, if you was here before – *with Nelson* – them tarts must be all frigging grandmas.'

'Hold yer wuish, man. Get on with it.'

The young men needed no urging. It had been a long boring week on the flying boat and as Ginger Kerrigan had expressed it an hour before, 'I've got a lot o' dirty water on my chest, mates, that needs to be got rid of toot-sweet. That's French for straight away. Luvverly grub!'

Now as CPO Ferguson posted himself primly on a chair next to the door with the remark, 'Nobody leaves without reporting to me, got it?' they broke ranks, pushing and shoving their way through the throng of sailors, to where the whores lined the stairs, rubbing their crotches, as if in the throes of unbearable passion or making obscene gestures with their tongues.

Ferguson sniffed. In his time he had frequented brothels all over the world. But now he was old and, as he was wont to remark to fellow CPOs in the petty officers' mess, 'It's nae dignified for them ratings to see a CPO rogering and rollicking and spending his bawbees on loose women. No good for the reputation of the Royal Navy, ye know.'

But now as he watched the scene: the naked Chinese waitresses hurrying back and forth with drinks and women of all colours, white, black, yellow, fondling the excited, red-faced young men, before a hurried scramble upstairs to the cubicles, he felt a kind of sad longing. 'Sandy,' he said to himself, 'it's been a damned long time since ye last dipped yer wick.'

A mile away from where CPO Ferguson was feeling the first stirrings of lust after such a long time, Smith, Bird and McIntyre were in conference with Mr Chen. As usual he was his customary oblique self, but he had provided them with the information they needed to plan their move on the morrow. Crouched in the half-light of the junk's single cabin which obviously had been built for the smaller-sized Chinese, with the blinded canary – blinded, according to Mr Chen, to make it sing louder – chirping in its cage in the corner, they ran through the plan once again. 'Once we have the pinnace, we set off for Fu Zhou, where according to Mr Chen,' he nodded at the Chinese and Mr Chen gave a slight bow in return, 'this war-lord chap General Wang controls the river. If the pirates are holding the Jap princess in that region, as your Mr Chen thinks they are,' again Mr Chen bowed, his bland face showing no emotion however, 'then we put the squeeze on him to get the pirates to release her.'

McIntyre rubbed his chin reflectively. 'He's a tough nut,' he said. 'I met him once. Tiny fat little feller with a squeaky high-pitched voice like a eunuch. There used to be a lot of them in old China. But he's got the power and he knows how to use it. Old China hands have told me that when the villagers use to refuse to pay the taxes he imposed – and he'd tax 'em for thirty years in advance–'

'Good Lord!' Dickie Bird exclaimed. 'He's worse than Lloyd George.'

McIntyre ignored the interruption. 'Well, he'd bury the women folk up to their necks in the earth and let the wild birds gradually peck out their eyes till the villagers decided it was wiser to pay the squeeze.'

Smith pulled a face, 'What cruelty!'

McIntyre shrugged. 'China *is* cruel. Always has been. Specially to women. Girl babies are routinely left naked to die or allowed to grow a bit and then sold to children's brothels.'

'But why doesn't the Nationalist Government in Nanking do something about it?' Smith objected.

'Because General Wang supports them and he *has* got an army of one hundred thousand or more. There are war-lords like him all over China. They pay lip-service to the government, but in reality they rule the roost themselves.' McIntyre raised his voice. 'Anyway, let's see what we can get out of him first!'

'Let me ask you one thing?' Smith said.

'Fire away.'

'Well, if these pirates are really holding the Jap princess, why haven't they sent a ransom note to – say – that Jap general who was going to marry her?'

McIntyre frowned. 'Agreed, it is strange. Yes, why?'

Mr Chen bowed slightly and said in that slightly sing-song accent of his, 'Possibly others factors are playing a role, eh?'

'What other factors?' McIntyre snapped.

Chen's round face revealed nothing. 'Perhaps the Japanese gentlemen are not wanting Lady Princess to be returned?' He smiled slightly and then shut up like a trap, leaving them to stare at him in bewilderment...

CPO Ferguson took out his old nickel watch, still marred by the dent caused by a piece of German shrapnel during the Battle of Jutland. He frowned. The men were still upstairs and their time was about to run out. 'Damned sassenachs,' he muttered grumpily under his breath. 'Nae discipline at all.'

Just then one of the White Russian whores – after the Revolution Shanghai had been swamped with them; Russian countesses and baronesses offering their aristocratic bodies for a handful of Chinese dollars – bent down in front of him. He gasped. She was naked under the sheer silk dress, which clung to her like a glove, and her pubes were clean shaven. Again CPO Ferguson felt that old lustful stirring of his loins. He flushed and wished the boys would get it over with and come down the damned stairs.

Now he flushed even more when the whore turned and looked directly at him in a bold challenging manner, as if she knew that he had just stared between her legs. 'You like?' she asked in delightfully accented English.

CPO Ferguson swallowed hard. 'Yes,' he admitted, 'I like.'

The whore lit a long Russian cigarette and puffed out the smoke, her eyes narrowed as she sized him up. Slowly, her breasts juggling provocatively under the sheer silk of her white dress, she advanced. 'You want more, sailor boy?'

CPO Ferguson hadn't been called 'sailor boy' since the turn of the century, but he couldn't find the words to protest, for with apparent casualness, her hand had dropped to his lap. Already he was beginning to harden under that gentle touch. He felt himself going even redder.

She blew smoke in his face and whispered huskily, 'You like fuckee-suckeee, sailor boy? Sonya take you once round the world. Only one sovereign, English.' She pouted her lips and thrust her breasts hard against the silk of her dress so that her nipples protruded excitingly.

'I ha nae much time,' Ferguson managed to gasp, licking his old lips which had become suddenly very dry.

'You have time for little Sonya?' she said. 'Do not disappoint me, sailor boy. I know what you have in the trousers. Make Sonya a little happy, eh.' She thrust her wet tongue into his right ear.

CPO Ferguson shivered and felt himself weakening rapidly. 'Och weel.' He gave in. 'I dinna want to hurt yer feelings, lassie. Come on then.'

Coming out of the whore's crib at the top of the stairs, busy fastening up his flies, Ginger Kerrigan caught a glimpse of the two of them disappearing into the blonde's crib. 'Well, blow me down,' he exclaimed to no one in particular, 'fancy old Chiefie, doing the two-backed beast at his frigging age. Bloody ought to be ashamed of hissen.' He saw Billy Bennett coming into the corridor and shouted above the din, 'I'm off for a pint of wallop, Billy.'

'D'yer think they've got any grub?' the fat sailor yelled back. 'Fancy something with chips. Allus hungry after a bit of the other.'

Ginger Kerrigan shook his head. 'Aint you got no soul? All that romance just now and all you can frigging well think of is frigging chips!'

'Shit carts,' Ginger Kerrigan said airily, as they pushed their way down the crowded street on their trip back to the junk, while the whores in the brothel hung out of the windows, waving and crying for them to come back soon. He indicated the two barefoot coolies who were stopping at regular intervals to rake up the faeces of the various animals that had passed this way.

'Don't have to tell me!' Billy Bennett exclaimed. 'What a frigging pong. What do they want the shit for?'

'Sell it to the farmers for their crops.'

'Ay,' CPO Ferguson broke his heavy silence, 'canny folks as I've already said. Family trade as well. They burn the inside of the nostrils o' their bairns with hot irons so that they canna smell a thing. Then when they're old enough, they take up the trade an' all.'

Billy Bennett shuddered. 'What a country! Fancy wanting to become a shitehawk.'

Ginger Kerrigan winked and said, 'But their womenfolk do know how to keep a sailor happy, don't they Chiefie? Best bit o' gash I've had in a month o' Sundays. How was yours, Chiefie?'

Ferguson scowled at the red-headed sailor. 'Ye mind yer own business,' he rasped. But inside he felt quite proud of himself. He'd given her a right rogering all right. She'd been panting and gasping and yelling for more – and that from a whore. And afterwards she'd asked where he was going and when he'd come back and see her again. He'd told her and then her cunning fingers had slipped down to his loins; and lo and behold it had worked again. 'Yes,' CPO Ferguson told himself proudly, 'there's still plenty o' piss and vinigar in ye yet, Archie Ferguson.'

Up in the brothel, Sonya stopped waving. She turned and put on her wrap. Followed by the suspicious eyes of 'Shanghai Lil' she went out to where she usually met her contact. With a bit of luck he'd give her the morphine she craved for her information. She knew he would pass it on to the hated Reds, who had ruined her family and her life. But she had to have that morphine. She quickened her pace and vanished into the growing darkness.

Chapter Five

It was dawn. The sun hung over the edge of the cliffs to the east like a big yellow ball. It cast its glowing light over the great river, already crowded with sampans and junks like their own. On the tow paths to both sides of the Yangtze, barefoot, sweating coolies tied together like slaves were dragging heavy sailless craft along, bent double, responding only to the harsh orders of the gangmasters.

Dickie Bird took another draw at the first cigarette of the day, balancing a cup of thin, milkless Chinese tea in his other hand, and said, 'What a performance, eh. Like something out of blessed ancient Rome, what.'

Smith at his side nodded wordlessly, as the Chinese sailors manning their junk, started to smoke too, only they weren't smoking tobacco. Instead they were pressing little balls of opium into their pipes. Smith told himself the toiling coolies on the river bank epitomized China for him. What a cruel country it was, a place where human life counted for nothing. He frowned at the thought and told himself the sooner this mission was over, the better. Even Withernsea on the East Yorkshire coast, where the crew of the *Swordfish* was usually based and which Ginger Kerrigan always called the 'arsehole of the world', seemed very attractive now after what he had seen of China.

'Morning.' It was McIntyre.

They returned his greeting and Smith told himself the big tough Canadian looked even grimmer than usual. 'Anything the matter?' he asked.

By way of an answer, McIntyre pointed his cigarette at the cliff to their right. 'Take a gander at that up there. Half an hour ago, Mr Chen spotted another one ... just like it.'

Dickie Bird stared at the column of still black smoke ascending slowly into the pale yellow dawn sky and said, 'A fire or something?'

'No,' McIntyre snapped in irritation. 'A goddam smoke signal. That's what Mr Chen says and he should know his Chinks if anybody does.'

'But why?' Smith asked quickly, realising

now why McIntyre was looking so grim.

'They're marking our progress down the river.'

'But who are?' Smith asked.

McIntyre shrugged a little carelessly. 'Who goddam knows? It could be Mr Chen's redbeards, you know the river pirates. It could be General Wang's guys. Anybody. But I think we'd better be prepared for trouble.' He reached into the pocket of his shabby raincoat and brought out an automatic. 'Yank Colt 45,' he announced, weighing the heavy pistol in the palm of his hand. 'Can stop a guy dead at fifty paces even if you hit him in the little finger. Something good that comes out of America at least. Mr Chen'll break them out to your guys once they've finished feeding their faces.'

'Oh my sainted aunt!' Dickie Bird exclaimed when he saw the big pistol. 'That thing really looks dangerous.'

'Shut up you fool,' Smith snapped, realising that Dickie was play-acting again, for his old friend had shot more than one man in his time. 'We'd better post watches then, Major.'

McIntyre nodded his agreement. 'I think it'd be better.' Then he walked back to the junk's solitary cabin to supervise the distribution of the guns.

By midday the beacons, if that was what they were, had been marking their progress for four hours and tension on the slow moving junk was mounting. 'Ye ken, it's like yon Chink water torture where they drop drips of water on yer head till yer go stark staring raving barmy. Hour after hour ... drip ... drip.' Ferguson relished his explanation, savouring the 'steady drip ... drip ... drip.'

Ginger Kerrigan gave a shudder. 'Put a sock in it, Chiefie,' he said. 'I'll be getting me monthlies if yer rabbit on like that.' He shivered again.

'Well, I'm only telling ye what I ken,' CPO Ferguson said and stared hard at the new column of smoke rising to their right. 'Ay, in my opinion now, it won't be long before the balloon goes up. Once we get in yon gorge ahead and into the shallows and slow down, then they'll strike. Mark my words.' With that he went back to his post, leaving Ginger and his shipmate Billy Bennett staring hard at the plume of black smoke, as if trying to see something there that was not visible to the others.

But when trouble came, surprisingly

enough it didn't come from the land at all. They were well within the gorge, picking their way through the traffic which had thickened in the shallows when the plane seemed to drop out of the narrow patch of sky above their heads. Instinctively they all looked up as it came thundering in below the level of the cliffs on both sides, the noise ear-splitting.

Smith recognized the type immediately. It was an old wartime Sopwith Camel two-seater. Now it was hurtling for them at about 100 mph. And there was no doubt the English-made plane was heading straight for them.

As the junk plodded on at its slow pace, Smith yelled above the racket, 'Take cover, chaps. He's heading for–' The rest of his words were drowned by the chatter of the twin machine guns mounted in front of the helmeted pilot. Scarlet flame stabbed the gloom of the gorge. Bullets plucked at the water all around the junk. Then the biplane was sailing into the sky, trailing smoke behind it.

McIntyre, in impotent rage, blazed away at it with his Colt for a few seconds before yelling, 'He's coming back in!'

Smith acted. He raced to the stern of the

junk, pushing the suddenly panicked coolies out of the way. He grabbed the great oar which acted as a rudder out of the oarsman's hands and, grunting, applied all his strength. The oaken paddle creaked under the strain. But it started to turn – slowly. Now the junk was creeping towards the lee of the great cliff.

Again the biplane came zooming in, its machine gun chattering. Slugs hit the water all around the junk. Coolies screaming with fear dived overboard and struck out for the shore. But now Smith, still pushing with all his strength at the oar, recognized a new danger. The observer clearly visible behind the pilot in the open cockpit, was tugging at a wire. Smith knew why. It was the toggle to unclink the little bombs lining the outer edge of the cockpit. 'Look out everybody!' he yelled desperately. 'He's going bomb us, the bastard!'

The first bomb came howling out of the sky. Smith held onto the oar grimly, willing it to turn faster so he could sail the junk into the protection of the cliff. It exploded only yards away. Water came hurtling over the side of the gunwale drenching him. He gasped and opened his mouth automatically as the next bomb hurtled downwards, shrieking a bansheelike howl. That way his eardrums wouldn't be punctured. It exploded on the tiny strip of sandy shore. A coolie shrieked and slapped into the water, his left leg severed by flying shrapnel. In an instant the water coloured a blood red.

Another bomb. The blast whipped across Smith's face like a slap from a flabby warm palm. He gasped as the detonation dragged the air from his lungs.

Now they were almost there. Up front, McIntyre standing erect, one hand behind his back, as if he were on some peacetime pistol range, was pumping shot after shot at the biplane.

Then it happened. As the biplane turned, seemingly barely missing the edge of the cliff, ready for another strafing run, the last of its bombs struck the keel of the junk. Shrapnel sang lethally through the air. Billy Bennett yelped in pain as he was hit in the shoulder. The junk lurched violently, as the ancient timber of its keel snapped apart. Almost immediately she began to sink.

'Abandon ship!' Smith yelled frantically. He let go of the steering oar as the junk began to list alarmingly.

The men needed no urging. They started to drop over the side into the shallow water which came up to their thighs in most cases.

'Look lively,' CPO Ferguson bellowed. 'Yon murdering bugger's coming in for the kill.' He threw himself over the side and started to wade through the water to the narrow strip of shingle beach.

Dickie Bird flashed Smith a look. Smith nodded for him to go, too. After all it was his privilege to be last off the craft. Then he was over the side as well, as the biplane raced along the floor of the gorge, machine guns chattering furiously. Angry flurries of water erupted to both sides of the lone figure wading through the shallows towards the safety of the beach. Suddenly Smith was overcome with anger. He stopped short and pulled out his Colt. In one and the same instant he aimed and fired. At that distance, as the biplane raced above, dragging its evil black shadows behind it on the water, he couldn't miss.

Great tears appeared in the canvas. The engine spluttered, stopped and then started again. Smith cursed. The bastard was getting away with it. Abruptly the engine spluttered once more and stopped for good. He looked at the pilot.

He was fighting the controls, eyes wild with fear behind the yellow goggles. To no avail! The tip of the biplane's wings caught the side of the cliff. Canvas and wood tore and splintered. The plane cartwheeled, disappeared over the top. Next instant there was a startlingly violet flash. The rumble of an explosion followed and as Smith paused there with the water of the Yangtze up to his knees, he could see the pall of black smoke slowly ascending to the afternoon sky, while the crew cheered and cheered.

It was only later, when they had rescued whatever they could of their personal possessions from the stranded junk, that McIntyre said in that harsh abrasive manner of his, 'I guess you saw the insignia of that plane?'

Dickie Bird shook his head, 'Can't say I did. I was too busy having a rather large funk.'

McIntyre looked at Smith enquiringly. The latter shook his head. 'Me neither.'

'Well, I'll tell you what it was. It was the old Oriental poached egg.'

'*What?*' the other two said in unison. 'The old rising sun. That's the emblem of Imperial Japan.'

Smith whistled softly and Dickie Bird asked, 'Well, what do you make of that?'

Mr Chen answered for his boss. 'Seemingly honourable Japanese gentlemen, do not want us to complete our journey.' He smiled winningly at the other three.

'But why?' Smith asked. 'Why are the Japs trying to stop us? After all we *are* trying to rescue their princess.'

But there was no answer forthcoming to that overwhelming question.

Chapter Six

'Dogs defile your great-grandmothers, all four of the chicken-defiling bags of dung!' the fat businessman spat defiantly at Mr Chen.

Mr Chen, apparently unmoved, smiled. He struck the fat sweating Chinese across the face once again, while behind him McIntyre covered the central room of the inn with his big Colt.

It was four hours now since they had climbed up the bank of the Yangtze and had spotted the new column of smoke rising a half a mile away. It was clear that someone had observed the failure of the Japanese plane to deal with them and was signalling anew to the unknown enemies. It was then that Smith and McIntyre made their hasty plan.

'My guess is that whoever lit the fire lives in that hamlet over there,' Smith said, pointing to the straggle of houses beyond the column of rising smoke. 'There's not a single house around otherwise and no trees. So the wood for the fire must have come from there.'

'Agreed,' McIntyre had said. 'So?'

'So, we'll keep on marching south-west, as if we suspect nothing, while you and Mr Chen here slip into the village and see if you can find out what the hell the mystery is.'

The inn lay in the centre of the hamlet with the chickens running through the dirt and the skinny-ribbed dogs barking somewhat fearfully at the two strangers. Scared barefoot children stared at McIntyre from the doorways of their straw-roofed huts, as if they had never seen a white man before, which was probably true.

McIntyre and Mr Chen ignored them and the hard looks that some of the peasants threw them. Like rich travellers, they thrust open the door of the inn to reveal a collection of benches and rosewood tables surrounded by lattice screens, the whole interior lit by half a dozen flickering hurricane lamps.

The place was empty save for an old woman with the old-style deformed feet and two very pretty girls standing looking bored in the shadows. Mr Chen ignored the girls. Instead he clapped his hands at the woman, ordered tea, beef with white vegetables, lotus root and rice.

The old woman gasped. Only very rich people could afford food like that. She hobbled away to carry out their orders, while in the shadows the bored girls had suddenly begun to smile winningly and stand more erect, thrusting out their breasts under the thin material of their dresses.

'What do you think, Mr Chen?' McIntyre asked, as they sipped the scalding hot tea, while they waited for the food to be cooked.

'I think it is possibly the affirmative. The rogues come from here.'

'But who's their leader?' McIntyre said a little angrily. 'Someone must pay them to light the signal columns.'

But before Mr Chen could give his opinion, the steaming bowls packed with meat, rice and vegetables together with the usual sauces, arrived and they set to it with their chopsticks, both suddenly realizing that they had not eaten since the previous day. Behind them the two girls started carrying brushwood and logs for the bathroom up the stairs, giggling sillily and throwing significant glances in the direction of the two men at the table as they did so. McIntyre knew what they were up to. But he concentrated on the food, for he still found it awkward to eat with chopsticks.

It was later, when they were naked in the stone tubs of hot water, each of them being attended to by the equally naked pretty girls from below, that the fat man entered. He frowned when he saw them there, especially when he saw the white man. 'What's the long nose doing here?' he snapped in Chinese. 'That kind of foreign devil ought to be defiled with dog dirt.'

The girl attending to McIntyre looked worried. A moment before she had been enjoyably rubbing his private parts with some kind of scented oil under the water, taking her time, as if it were all part of a ritual. Now she took her hands away sharply, as if McIntyre's hardness had burnt her.

The fat man clapped his hands and tugged at the neck of his shirt impatiently. Hurriedly the other girl dried her hands and padded wetly across the floor to undress him. McIntyre flashed Mr Chen a quick look. As usual Mr Chen's bland round face revealed nothing, but he closed one eye for a fraction of a second. McIntyre knew what that meant. This was their man.

Totally neglected now, with their water rapidly growing cold, the two clambered out, as one of the girls raced downwards, still naked, to fetch fresh wood for the *k'ang*. It was ten minutes later, when the fat man had begun to wallow in his bath, looking very pleased with himself as both girls dealt with his body, and they were dressed, that Mr Chen acted. He strode over to where the man, slowly going a beetroot red with the heat and the attentions underwater of the girls, lay. Drawing back his hand, he slapped the fat man across the face.

The girls shrieked and the fat man cried, 'Why did you do that?' Mr Chen hit him again, while a watching McIntyre drew out his Colt.

'You smell of smoke,' Mr Chen told him. 'The smell has still not gone.' Without violence he knocked the bottle of scented oil from the side of the stone tub. 'Even the oil does not hide the stink.'

'You are impudent,' the fat man answered.

Obviously he was not afraid, even of the big pistol. 'You have worked too long for the foreign devil. He who is trimmed down below like a Turk.' He indicated McIntyre who was circumcised.

Mr Chen translated quickly and McIntyre knew this was their man. How else would the fat Chinese know about their relationship? 'Right Mr Chen, let's find out who pays him to light these signals.'

Routinely and without rancour, Mr Chen hit the fat man once more. The fat man spat at him, but Chen dodged the spittle easily. He posed his question.

The fat man looked at Chen scornfully. 'Do you think I'd tell you, you filthy weasel. You toad.' He stared up at Mr Chen defiantly. 'May dogs defile your unborn children!'

Mr Chen put his hand beneath the surface of the water, found the fat man's flaccid organ, grunted and twisted hard. The fat man shrieked and would have shot upright with the intense pain if it had not been for the fact that Mr Chen was holding him fast with his other hand. 'Now,' he said, 'you talk, or else.' He squeezed the man's testicles a little harder.

The fat man's face turned the colour of

puce. His eyes bulged from his sweat-lathered face, 'Yes, yes, I talk,' he choked. 'Please no more ... *please!*'

Mr Chen relaxed his grip a little. 'Who paid you?' he snapped with unusual directness for him.

McIntyre tensed. Now they were getting a little closer to solving the mystery of the missing princess. If he could learn what role Captain Moto played in the business– He stopped short. His sixth sense told him that something was wrong. He could see it in the eyes of the naked girls as they stared out over his back into the hamlet beyond.

'It is the Jap–' the fat man began in the same instant that the burst of machine-gun fire scythed through the room. One of the girls screamed. A neat red hole had suddenly appeared in her trim yellow left breast. Slowly she began to sink to her knees, as Mr Chen released his hold on the fat man and grabbed for his Colt.

McIntyre spun round. Down below a ragged collection of peasants were massing, crying and swearing. Some had bamboo staves with curved knives tied to them. Others had ancient curved muskets. But some had more modern German Mausers and it was these men who were doing the firing under the orders of a small bespectacled man mounted on a white pony. The man was dressed in European clothes, including a somewhat foolish looking trilby hat. But there was no mistaking him. 'Christ, Captain Moto,' McIntyre snarled and, dropping to his right knee, while next to him the wounded Chinese girl writhed and twisted in pain on the wet floor, started snapping off aimed shots to left and right through the open window. A moment later Mr Chen joined him. His face as expressionless as ever, he started to fire too.

A peasant went down, his hands clawing the air as if he were trying to climb the rungs of an invisible ladder. The others backed off. On the horse, Moto shouted at them angrily, raising his riding crop, as if he were tempted to beat them. But still the barefoot peasants hesitated. Some even went to ground behind a rickety hay cart and started firing from the prone position.

Again slugs pattered against the walls, hewing out chunks of plaster and timber. The unwounded girl screamed and dropped to the floor, too. Whether she had been wounded or not, McIntyre couldn't see. He was too busy changing his magazine, as Moto urged the peasants on to attack again.

'Chen, we know that Moto is involved. But why?' McIntyre called over his shoulder as he started firing once more. 'Hurry up, find out why Moto's in this bus–' He stopped short.

The fat man lay slumped in the water, which was slowly turning pink, a hole drilled into the centre of his forehead. And McIntyre didn't need a crystal ball to know the Chinese was dead.

He made his decision. 'We're getting out, Mr Chen,' he snapped hastily. 'No use wasting any more time here.' He reached up to his full height and grabbed at the ceiling, hammering it with the butt of his pistol. Plaster and wood began raining down.

McIntyre knew his Chinese houses. The ceilings under the straw roofs were simply a thin layer of wattle and cane. They'd get out through the roof. Next to him Chen nodded his silent approval and kept on firing.

In a matter of minutes a sweat-lathered, anxious McIntyre had carved a hole big enough for them to crawl through. 'Quick,' he gasped and bent at the knees.

Mr Chen didn't need to be told what to do. As McIntyre commenced firing again – blindly this time – he clambered up onto McIntyre's back and thrust himself through the hole. A moment later he had disappeared into the space between the ceiling and roof.

Behind him, McIntyre flung one last glance at the courtyard below, firing as he did so. Moto was rallying the peasants, laying about him with his crop, slashing backs to left and right. McIntyre knew they'd attack soon. He looked at the two girls, huddling together naked as they were, the one still bleeding from her wounded breast. He guessed they wouldn't survive long once the peasants stormed the inn. But they'd rape them first which might give him and Chen a bit of a start. Then he hesitated no longer. He heaved himself into the space between the roof and ceiling and was gone, leaving the girls huddled in each other's arms like star-crossed lovers.

Chapter Seven

'Hungry ghosts, we say,' Mr Chen said, with surprising directness for him.

'What ... what's a hungry ghost?' Dickie Bird asked, as the column slogged on through the afternoon heat heading for the spot on the Yangtze where they would meet the gunboat.

By way of an answer, Mr Chen pointed across the rocky flats shimmering in blue waves with the heat. 'Unexpected visitors.'

'Oh my sainted aunt!' Dickie Bird exclaimed and then he said hurriedly to Smith, 'I say Smithie, there's somebody coming. Look, old chap.'

The column stumbled to a weary halt as they turned to survey the distant black spots.

'I can't make them out,' Billy Bennett said.

Gently Ginger Kerrigan patted him on the shoulder. 'Eyes gone,' he explained. 'I've told him time and time agen to stop bashing his bishop. But would he listen? Would he hellus. Now his eyes has gone. Years o' self-abuse.'

'None of that filthy talk,' CPO Ferguson snapped, as Smith focused his field glasses and a dozen or so riders mounted on little ponies slid into the circles of calibrated glass. He saw the rifles slung over their shoulders and he said in alarm, 'Whoever they are, they're armed. Stand by, lads.'

'Fuck this for a tale,' Billy Bennett said

ponderously. 'I ain't had nothing to eat all day and now they expect me to fight.'

'Pick up thee musket, Sam,' Ginger Kerrigan mimicked the music hall comedian, drawing his own Colt, 'and stop bleeding moaning.'

Now they waited tensely as the riders got closer and closer. They had formed up behind a ridge of broken rock which seemed to offer the best cover, each man crouched with his pistol at the ready, and each wrapped in a cocoon of his own private fears and apprehensions. For it seemed even to the most unimaginative of the *Swordfish*'s crew that they were lost and very vulnerable in this huge strange land, in which they could easily disappear without trace and no one would be the wiser.

By now the riders had spotted them and were urging their ponies to move more swiftly, as their leader rose in his spurs and pointed in the direction of the waiting sailors. McIntyre flashed a look at Mr Chen. The latter shrugged, as if he didn't know either what to make of the riders. Were they friendly or not?

Smith said, 'Hold your fire, lads. They might not attack.' All the same he raised his Colt and aimed at the riders' leader. He looked lean and tough, his skinny chest criss-crossed with leather bandoliers of cartridges, a sword dangling from his waist, with a rifle thrust into the bucket at his knee. Smith told himself he and the rest of his band looked very professional. But why were they riding straight at the waiting men like this? It could mean suicide for them if the *Swordfish* crew opened fire once they were within range, which would be very soon.

Suddenly, a little startlingly, the leader tugged at the bit of his mount and flung up his free hand. The riders stopped dead. Slowly, the only sound the metallic clink of his harness, the Chinese started to come towards them, while his men waited.

'Shall I drop his nibs now, sir?' Ginger Kerrigan, who had the keenest eyesight of them all, asked in a tense whisper.

'No, hold on,' Smith commanded. 'We don't want to start a barney if it's not necessary.' He turned to Mr Chen. 'What do you think, Mr Chen?'

'I think from what I can see of his uniform,' the latter replied, 'it is possible we might be dealing with a Nationalist.'

McIntyre grunted. 'They're all bandits whatever uniform they wear,' he said sourly.

Suddenly the rider halted perhaps some fifty yards away. He stood up in his stirrups, as if he wanted to get a better view of the men lying crouched behind the rocks. 'You are the British sailors?' the rider asked in fair English. 'I am Captain K'uang. I have been sent to find you.'

'I say!' Dickie Bird exclaimed. 'For such a villainous-looking chappie, he speaks pretty decent English, what.'

'Shut up, Dickie,' Smith said hastily. 'Who sent you, Captain?'

The Chinese captain said, 'Nanking. You have had trouble with bandits, I hear. We dealt with them this dawn.' He patted the flank of his mare and Smith gasped. For the first time he saw what was hanging there: two severed heads attached to the harness by their hair! The Chinese captain saw their looks and said swiftly, 'It is the only way with bandits – fire with fire.'

McIntyre shot Mr Chen a significant look. It said:

'How the devil does Nanking know about us?'

Mr Chen's face showed no emotion. But his clever brain was racing. The Japanese Army in China was obviously involved in this business of the kidnapped princess.

Somehow the Nationalist Government in Nanking had become aware of what was going on. Why should they send out Captain K'uang's patrol to find them? He sniffed. He didn't like puzzles, especially ones he didn't seem able to solve. But he kept his peace and watched carefully, as the Captain summoned his riders to come closer, noting as they did so that each horse carried its share of severed heads, but that they were all those of Chinese. Captain Moto obviously had escaped.

An hour later they were sheltering under some trees, the first they had seen since the junk had sunk, eating cold rice covered with a fish sauce that stank to high heaven, but which tasted very good, supplied to them by the soldiers. There were also large mugs of rice wine, of which Ginger Kerrigan commented happily, 'It ain't exactly wallop, Billy, but it's wet and it's got a kick.'

Billy Bennett didn't reply, but then the fat sailor was eating, and that process always occupied his attention fully.

Squatting to the rear of the Chinese riders who were eating themselves and were being gently pumped by a smiling Mr Chen, Smith avoided looking at the severed heads, as he said softly, 'Let's try to sort this out, chaps. One,' he ticked the point off on his finger, 'the Japs are involved. Why, we don't know. All we know is that they don't want the princess rescued. Two,' again he ticked off the point on his fingers, 'the Chinese Nationalists are in the know. But again we don't know what their interest in the matter is, though they seem to be helping us. Three,' he ticked off the point, 'these Chinese Nationalists might help us put pressure on this warlord, General Wang.'

'Maybe,' McIntyre said a little doubtfully.

'Mr Smith.'

Smith turned a little startled. It was Mr Chen who had crept up on them in that noiseless manner of his, as if he always walked on the tips of his toes.

'What is it, Mr Chen?'

'There is another item for your count.'

'Another?'

'Yes, Number Four.' Chen ticked off the number on his fingers, whether seriously or in imitation of Smith – Chinese humour was strange to them – they didn't know. 'Captain K'uang was not just looking for those peasant bandits who attacked you.' He lowered his voice even more. 'I've been talking to his men.'

'Go on,' Smith urged.

'Four is the Communists.'

Smith groaned and Dickie Bird said, 'Oh not more of the blessed chaps.' He clapped his head, as if in pain. 'The jolly old bean is really spinning with all this Sherlock Holmes mystery stuff.'

'What about the Communists, Mr Chen?' Smith rasped, silencing Dickie with a stern look. 'What role do they play in this?'

Mr Chen shrugged slightly. 'Common soldier, he knows nothing. It is understood.' He shrugged again. 'But Captain K'uang does. It is my opinion that he – and his masters – are possibly afraid what the Communists may do to the princess if they can find and take her from the redbeards.'

'What exactly?' Smith asked quickly.

'Rape ... murder ... publicly by Chinese low-caste persons.'

'To what purpose, Mr Chen?'

'I am a simple humble man,' Mr Chen commenced, lowering his clever brown eyes.

McIntyre laughed a little scornfully. 'Simple ... humble,' he repeated. 'That'll be the day.'

Mr Chen did not seem to hear. 'But it is my belief that the defiling and murder of the princess will create an incident, a very useful one for the Communists.'

'How do you mean?' Smith asked.

'If the Japanese gentlemen use it to start a fight with the Chinese Nationalists–' Mr Chen left the rest of the sentence unsaid. But Smith knew what he meant. He remembered C's words back in a rainy London, and despite the heat of the day he felt that same cold finger of apprehension trace its way down his spine. He shivered.

'A ghost run over your grave, Smithie?' Dickie Bird asked lightly.

'Something like that.' Smith raised his voice. 'The sooner we get on to this the better,' he said, face set and determined. 'Mr Chen, we'll break camp now and set off for the rendezvous with the – er – *Cockchafer* before dark. Would you tell Captain K'uang that. I don't know whether he wants to accompany us any further, but we're going.' Smith grunted, 'and tell him thank you for his assistance.'

Mr Chen rose to carry out his task, while CPO Ferguson roused the men, who finished off the last of their rice and fish paste swiftly. They, too, didn't want to spend another night on these barren heights above the Yangtze, especially Billy Bennett who, licking the last of the fish paste off his fingers (for none of them had been able to eat with chopsticks) said, 'Ay the sooner we get back to some proper vittels – bully and bangers – the better.'

'Christ, you've just bloody well scoffed a–' Ginger Kerrigan began and then decided it wasn't worth it. Billy, he told himself, had a passionate love affair with his belly and nobody would ever come between the two.

For a little while Captain K'uang's cavalry trotted at the side of the sailors, those horrible dead men's heads bobbing up and down with the motions of their shaggy ponies. Then as the great river came into view once more, with far down below the sight of two gleaming white craft which could belong only to the Royal Navy, the lean hard-faced Chinese Captain reined in his mount and said to Smith, 'Well, now you are safe – as safe as you will ever be in China.' He gave a faint smile and Smith smiled back up at him, thinking that the Captain's words were meant as a mild form of a joke. Later he was to find out they weren't.

Quite formally they shook hands and then K'uang rasped a command in Chinese and he and his riders turned and started to trot inland. For a moment or two the sailors stared after the departing cavalrymen. Then they turned and, forcing the pace a little, they set off down the cliff to where they belonged – the water.

Chapter Eight

'She's nae *Swordfish*, mind ye,' CPO Ferguson announced, eying the gleaming white pinnace, as if she were a thoroughbred horse. 'But she's a bonny enough wee thing.'

Smith narrowed his eyes against the glare of the sun rising above the Yangtze and stared at the craft which they were now going to take over. Next to him the young sub-lieutenant who had been sent over from the *Cockchafer* to guide them round their new home, a very junior officer who was obviously awed by Smith's Victoria Cross, said, 'The RAY had to reach a compromise with the design, sir. On one hand the vessel had to have a very shallow draft. On the other hand there were weapons to be carried and enough accommodation provided for a landing party when we had to go in and sort the Chinks,' he saw Mr Chen and added hastily, 'Chinamen … out.'

Smith nodded his understanding. If the pinnace was too heavy, it wouldn't have been able to sail the shallower waters of the Yangtze.

'Anyway, finally, sir,' the sub-liuetenant continued, 'a specification was worked out, giving her a draught of two feet.'

Smith whistled softly at such a shallow draught and Dickie Bird proclaimed, 'We'll be skimming over the dizzy bottom.'

'She's got a speed of twelve knots, not as fast the skimmers you used in the war, sir,' the sub-lieutenant said, 'but she has six hundred miles of endurance, accommodation for a small crew plus a ten-man boarding party. Armament is twin Lewis guns,' he pointed to the two ugly-looking machine guns just behind the bridge on the monkey island, 'and one six pounder quick-fired forrard.' He paused and then said rather lamely, 'That's about it, sir.'

Smith thanked him and said, 'Perhaps you'd show CPO Ferguson the engine room, in case there's something new.'

'Well, I mean Chiefie is really used to sails,' Ginger Kerrigan said cheekily, 'that's how they trained 'em in Nelson's days.'

The old Scot flashed him a look, but said nothing. He was too eager to look at the new engines, for engines were his greatest joy.

While the two went down below, Smith wasted no time. 'All right, duty watch get to your stations. I want us out of here and underway in two hours. There's heaps of daylight ahead of us yet.'

'Wise,' McIntyre agreed. 'On the Yangtze at night it's best to batten down the hatches, or whatever the Navy does, and keep an eye open for pirates.'

'You're probably right, Major,' Smith said. 'The captain of the – er – *Cockchafer* – God I'll never get used to the name of that vessel – has told me that the pinnace is provisioned for at least two weeks. Ammo lockers are filled chock-a-block as well. No problems there. He's also provided me with five hundred Horsemen of St George,' he meant gold sovereigns, 'which we can use for further supplies etc, if necessary. In other words we are totally independent. We have wireless-telegraphy, to be used in an emergency. But RAY prefers us not to use it unless absolutely necessary. That way the Japs and the Chinese – for that matter all parties – won't be able to trace us.' He looked around the circle of their keen young faces, telling himself that he could trust everyone of them implicitly. 'We're on our way. Now everything depends on us – and luck.'

'The game's afoot, Watson, eh,' Dickie Bird said enthusiastically. 'The thrill of the chase and all that.'

McIntyre was not impressed. He said, 'Yeah, and someone else knows it as well.'

'What?' Smith exclaimed.

'Look up there.' McIntyre pointed the end of his cigarette up to the heights.

They narrowed their eyes against the glint of the sun and stared in that direction. A bright light winked on and off, though the light did not move.

'What do you make of it?' Smith asked.

'Somebody's watching us – somewhat carelessly – through binoculars,' the big Canadian answered. 'And your ordinary little yellow Oriental usually doesn't possess field glasses, do you think?'

'No,' Smith agreed. He puffed out his lips in a gesture of exasperation. 'What a country. All right, let's get this show on the road.'

McIntyre stared up at the heights once more as the men started to bustle about their duties on the trim new craft and from below came the sudden throb of engines as

CPO Ferguson started them up. The light had vanished. But he knew they were still being watched. He could feel it. 'Dammit,' he cursed to himself, instinctively feeling in his pocket for his pistol.

Mr Chen's dark eyes followed the movement. He said quietly, 'The Major is pretty right to think thus.'

McIntyre turned slightly startled and saw Chen looking at where he had buried his hand in his pocket. He forced a tight smile. 'Ah, Mr Chen, they'll have to get up earlier in the morning if they're going to catch us out, eh?'

Mr Chen said nothing and McIntyre could see he wasn't convinced. For the first time since Mr Chen had come to work for him, he could tell the Chinese was worried.

Two miles away Captain K'uang rode into the shabby hamlet with half a troop. He had left the rest to watch the boat down below on the Yangtze. His lean face wrinkled in contempt at the sight of the place: sickly children, mostly naked, skinny-ribbed dogs and filthy women. What a bunch, he told himself. They scraped enough food together in the summer to keep themselves in the winter, huddled together underground, half-starved and frozen, probably copulating with their animals. 'These are my people,' he said to himself, hawking and spitting over the side of his mount with contempt. Kill half the population of China and a new people would emerge, hard, proud and fit, ready to work for a better life.

He stopped the first peasant he came across directly in the dirt track that led through the tumbledown place. They had got rid of the heads of the government soldiers they had killed to obtain their uniforms so as not to frighten the peasants. But, the woman, already going bald, suckling a naked infant from her sagging dug, was scared all the same. 'Where's the merchant?' he demanded, knowing there'd be only one in a place like this. 'We need supplies.'

Hurriedly the frightened woman told him, the baby wearily sucking at her breast, as if it already knew there was no milk there. He urged his horse forward and the others followed, grinning with anticipation. There'd be rice wine to loot, they told themselves, and then they'd rape the women, as ugly as they were. Still they were holes. That was all that counted in their rough-tough lives: always on the move, living in constant fear that they would be discovered. Then it would be the usual torture to make them sing, emasculation and beheading. They had to live life day by day, despite Comrade K'uang's reassurances that one day they would have a better life than this.

The merchant was fat and frightened. He put out his opium pipe immediately he saw the tall lean captain striding out of the sunshine into the smelly darkness of his little store, the ceiling hung with dried fish and smoked ducks. K'uang didn't waste words. He knew the type. He flung a wad of looted and worthless Nationalist banknotes on the table top in front of the merchant. 'That will pay for what my men take,' he rasped. His eyes took in the girl hiding behind the beaded curtain to the rear of the counter. 'I pay extra for the woman,' he added.

'But the notes have no worth, Honourable Captain,' the merchant quavered, 'and that is my daughter. She is only thirteen, sir.' He wrung his pudgy hands together. Contemptuously K'uang noted that the little nail of each hand had been allowed to grow to an enormous length in the manner of the Mandarin class. This was to indicate that he did not work with his hands like the peasants.

'She's old enough, defiler of dogs,' K'uang snapped. 'Get out my way.'

'But sir,' the merchant said, weakly trying to stop him.

'Sucker of horse cocks!' K'uang bellowed, his eyes gleaming dangerously, as he dropped his hand to his pistol. 'Out of my way.'

The merchant gave in, silent tears rolling down his fat cheeks, as the soldiers started to loot his store for supplies and rice wine.

The girl fought silently. She didn't attempt to scream. She knew no one would come and help her. He fought back, face already flushed with lust and triumph. He pulled off her trousers. Then he ripped open her shirt. It fell from her. Her breasts were small and firm, tipped a delicate pink. The sight increased his mounting lust. He held onto her with one hand and fumbled with the flies of his looted army breeches.

Then she was naked. She held her hands across the faint wisp of brown hair at the base of her stomach. The tears streamed down her face and she struggled no more. She was going to let it happen like all Chinese women did in the end.

For a minute he felt pity for her. But then he remembered the women in his own village as a boy; how the landlords and merchants seized girls as young as twelve and made them suck cock; how the poor ate sand and grass to keep alive until their bones dissolved and they died.

He pushed her hands away. 'Darling,' he said almost cheerfully, 'this is your wedding day, so you might as well enjoy it.' With both hands he forced her legs apart and lifted her at the same time, his breath coming in sharp, harsh gasps, as he anticipated the pleasure to come. Then he brought her down hard. She screamed shrilly as he impaled her, ripping and tearing at the flesh as he forced his full length inside her.

The raped girl and her father were both locked up in the inner room and both were still sobbing. Outside some of the men were getting a little drunk on rice wine. K'uang knew that the villagers had already fled. They could guess what the soldiers would want after they had drunk enough. That's why he had locked the girl away with her father. He was satisfied. He didn't want her to be raped by the rest of the half-troop. That would be too much. Besides he knew that at least two of them had syphilis.

Then he forgot the girl, the villagers, his men and concentrated on the task at hand. He had taken the merchant's ink and brushes to write the letter. It would have been easier in English and he would have written the letter with his prized fountain pen, the Waterman that the missionaries had given him at the mission school as their prize pupil.

But his chief in Nanking had always maintained he did not speak English, though K'uang felt he did. With him it was either Chinese or Russian and K'uang did not know the latter language. So laboriously he set about the brush strokes on the fine rice paper. 'Comrade Borodin,' he wrote, 'I have followed up the information from our agent in Shanghai. The English of whom you have knowledge are looking for...'

In the locked room, the raped girl was still sobbing. But her father, the merchant, had long ceased. Now he was calculating how high her dowry would have to be to get rid of her since she was no longer a virgin.

Chapter Nine

Borodin slit the seal and opened the message the courier had just brought him. Outside in the Street of the Three Unhappy Brides a Chinese funeral was taking place.

Hordes wailed. Men banged away at their drums, giving off solemn hollow notes. Mourners keened and beggars attracted to a rich funeral like flies were wailing for alms.

Borodin hardly noticed. By now he had become accustomed to the endless noise of Chinese cities. Now he concentrated on the message from Comrade K'uang, reading it once and then re-reading it carefully for a second time in case he had missed anything important.

He was a small, slightly portly man with a balding head, compensated by a rich brown beard. He could have been any nationality, except Russian, though he purported to be of that nationality. There was nothing Slavic about his sallow, hook-nosed features.

Outside the mourners were letting off firecrackers. He jumped, startled. He had never liked the sound of explosions, although he had taken part in the Revolution back in 1917 and had heard gunfire enough in his time. Still he hated the noise and the resultant bloodshed of firing. He left it to people like K'uang to carry out that side of the business for him.

Now he concentrated on the import of the message he had just received from K'uang, thinking it through and how he would report it to Aronson in Leningrad. Officially he was an agent of the Comintern but, in reality, Aronson in Leningrad with his finger in every pie, gave him his orders.

In this year of 1927, he knew Russia was threatened on all sides. Internally the nation was on the verge of starving, with the possibility of a second revolution starting at any moment. Externally, the Mother Country was being challenged by the great powers, such as Britain and Germany, even France, which would dearly love to see the downfall of Russian Communists. As Aronson always maintained in his talks with Borodin, 'The only way we can save Russia at the present time is to keep those who wish our downfall occupied with troubles in their own backyard.' Now he reasoned a conflict between China and Japan over this missing Jap princess would do just that. In addition, it would open the way, in the end, for a Chinese Communist take-over in this vast country. Then Russia would have a powerful ally to its east and create a buffer zone against the machinations of Japanese and Chinese Imperialists.

He nodded and mind made up, clapped his hands in the Chinese fashion. Chien, his boy, appeared as if by magic. Chien was exceedingly handsome with his smooth yellow skin, plucked eyebrows and red-painted lips. At night Borodin would often ask him to dress up in women's clothes and put on the wig they had had specially made for him. Then the young man looked a perfect girl.

But despite his lips and affected feminine gestures, Chien was brave and resourceful. Twice Chien had been captured by the Nationalists and had been tortured. But he had refused to speak and betray his master-lover, even when they had rammed a bamboo stave up his anus to ruin his sphincter; and twice he had been clever enough to escape.

'Master?' Chien asked, flashing him a warm smile with those beautiful teeth of his and bowing slightly.

Borodin returned his smile and answered, 'I want you to memorize this message, Chien. It is to be given to Comrade Chairman personally. You understand – no one else?'

Again his young lover bowed.

'Tell him that Comrade Chan K'uang is following the English. In due course they will lead us to this Japanese Imperialist woman. Once we have located her, the

Comrade Chairman must send the Squad of Sudden Death.'

Chien was impressed by the mention of the ruthless killers who had made the whole of China tremble with their bold and murderous exploits.

'She must be eliminated immediately before there is any attempt to rescue her. It will be the incident we have long been waiting for. Clear?'

'Yes, Master.'

Borodin crooked his finger towards the handsome youth.

He followed the unspoken command and came forward. Borodin said softly, 'Take the greatest care of yourself, my boy. Remember you will have to pass through the frontline of those dogs, the Nationalists. They're always on the lookout for our spies and agents. And I would hate,' Borodin's voice quavered, 'to lose you, my dear.'

Chien smiled boldly. 'They won't catch me, Master.'

'Well said. Now, my dear, you may kiss me.'

Borodin leaned forward tenderly, as Chien embraced, him, slipping his tongue between the other man's open lips. The latter felt a thrill of passion sweep through him, but he contained himself. There was still work to be done.

He waited for five minutes after Chien had left to be quite sure that he was alone in the house. Outside the long funeral procession was still moving by. The drums banged and the horns blared as the scores of ragged beggars yelled for money at the rich mourners in their sedan chairs.

Then he was satisfied that there was no one else in the house. He walked across to the tall lacquered cupboard on the far wall. With the special key that never left his person, even when he slept (for he knew that if the authorities ever found what was in there it would automatically mean his death by beheading) he opened it and stepped inside, closing the door behind him.

In the gloom, he moved aside the coats and other clothes that the big cupboard contained, fumbling for the others hidden keyhole to the cupboard's rear. He found it and unlocked it too. A moment later he stepped into the tiny airless room, which was the heart of his espionage ring in Nationalist-held China.

Here was the great safe which contained the gold coins he used for bribes; the passports of half a dozen different countries, all with the same picture, his own; the safe conducts signed by warlords, who really ruled Nationalist China; the silencers he gave to his agents when they had to carry out a political assassination, and the radio with which he signalled Leningrad and his boss, Aronson: a radio that even Beria, the head of the NKVD*, knew nothing about. One look in that safe by an investigator and his fate would be sealed, Borodin told himself. For it would tell the investigator that it belonged to the man who ran Communist espionage inside China.

He opened the safe, took out the radio and set it up on the tiny desk against the wall. Swiftly he attached it to the aerial concealed inside the wall that led right up to the roof, for the message he was going to send would travel right across Asia into European Russia, to far off Leningrad. And that message would have to be brief. He didn't want it to be picked up by Beria's detector men. That could lead to awkward, possibly dangerous questions.

He switched on and felt the small radio

---

* Beria was the head of the Soviet Secret Police, the NKVD, the forerunner of the present-day KGB.

throb with power – he had recharged the glass-walled accumulators which powered it the previous day himself. He nodded his head in approval and in the manner of solitary men who spoke to themselves, said, 'Very good. . . very good indeed.'

Now he picked up the headphones and gave his call sign, once, twice, three times. They were alert at the other end in Leningrad. A faint voice, distorted and crackling said, 'Ready?'

Swiftly, but clearly, so that they could be no mistake, he said the message, *'Operation Kill Jap Princess has commenced.'*

At the other end, the faint voice said, *'Horoscho.'* The radio went dead.

For a moment Borodin sat there smiling faintly. 'Good,' he repeated the word, 'good indeed.' Then he started to put the radio and the rest back into the safe, pleased with himself.

The stage was set, the actors were in place, the drama could commence.

PART TWO

The River Of Life And Death

Chapter One

The Japanese gunboat slid out of the mist hovering above the great river and caught them by surprise. It was going very slowly and the damp clinging mist had muted the sound of its engines. Now there it was, powerful and somehow sinister with a large awning covering the big gun on the foredeck and any crew who might have been there, too.

Hastily Smith had the jack lowered as was the naval custom, the smaller ship saluting the larger one. But there was no response from the Japanese vessel. The rising sun flag remained firmly on its mast and there seemed to be no officer about to return McIntyre's salute.

'I say, like a deuced ghost ship, what?' Dickie Bird chortled, as the gunboat slid by them, hardly churning the water, no sign of life on its upper deck.

Angrily McIntyre let his hand fall from his cap. 'But the little Nip bastards are there all right. Up on the bridge,' he snorted. 'They're up to something – you can bet your bottom dollar on that.'

'But they're only patrolling the river, just as our chaps do,' Smith objected.

'No sir,' McIntyre answered. 'Their gunboats haven't left the general area of Shanghai for weeks now. They're concentrating there for the time when the balloon goes up.'

For a while they were silent, watching the big craft slip back into the mist until finally it was gone, with not even the sound of its engines audible any more. It was as if the gunboat had never even existed.

Smith thought about Dickie's 'ghost ship' remark. There *was* something ghostlike about the Japanese craft, and the thought made him uneasy. He made a decision. He turned to Dickie Bird. 'I think we'll order the off-duty watch back on deck, Dickie,' he said slowly, as if he were thinking out the words as he spoke them.

Dickie Bird shot him a quick look. 'Something wrong, old bean?'

'I don't know exactly, Dickie. But that Jap boat–' he left the rest of his words unspoken.

Now a heavy brooding silence descended upon the pinnace as it threaded its way at a snail's pace through the fog-shrouded river. Now and again the silence was broken by the mournful hoot of some ship's siren far off, but otherwise there was little traffic on the great river. Smith reasoned that the locals had been put off by the fog – the Yangtze was dangerous at such times for the Chinese who sailed without charts designating the many dangers of the river – but in his mind he knew there was something else. Perhaps the Chinese had been warned off the river on this particular day. But why and of what? He had no answer to those two questions.

Time passed leadenly, as the men on watch, manning the guns or standing double lookout, slowly grew cold and damp in the fine wet mist which penetrated everything. Ginger Kerrigan moaned to Billy Bennett, 'Yer'd think this was the frigging North Sea and frigging Withernsea instead of the tropics.' He shivered dramatically.

'But this ain't the tropics, Ginger,' Billy objected, pudgy hand searching his pockets in case there was something there to be eaten, but his old shipmate wasn't listening.

Time passed, even more slowly, as the morning gave way to a cold drizzly afternoon. Smith had hot tea with rum served, and the steaming hot brew with its powerful kick cheered the men up for a while, but eventually the effects wore off and Smith began to wonder whether he had done right to have stood the whole crew to.

Obviously Dickie Bird felt the same, for he said, staring out of the bridge with the drizzle streaming down the glass like bitter, cold tears, 'Bit much, Smithie, you know. In brass monkey weather like this—' He stopped short and exclaimed, 'Hello, hello!'

'What is it?' Smith asked sharply.

'To port, it's our Nip friend again.'

Smith swung round. Bird was right. The big Japanese gunboat was stationary, apparently at anchor at the entrance to what Smith took to be one of the typical gorges they had found elsewhere on the Yangtze – steep cliff like banks on both sides with the water racing in a wild white fury through them.

'That's strange,' McIntyre, who was with them on the bridge, commented. 'Why have the Nips anchored there?'

'Search me, old thing,' Dickie Bird answered, his face equally as puzzled. 'The Japs must have been this way before. They can't surely be scared of navigating a stretch of wild water. Still,' he shrugged, 'nothing to do with us.' He looked at Smith.

The latter shrugged. 'Nothing much we can do about it, you're right there, Dickie, but there's definitely something fishy about this whole set up. Look she doesn't even have riding lights.'

It was true. There was not a single light visible on the Japanese craft although darkness was falling rapidly.

At the controls CPO Ferguson automatically started to raise the speed of the pinnace without being ordered to. Smith didn't object. He too reasoned the sooner they passed the Japanese vessel and got through the narrows, the better.

Again they sailed by the strangely silent Japanese boat, and again Smith felt that same sensation of being watched by many unseen eyes.

Once more the Japanese ship disappeared into the wet gloom, but no longer were they alone on the river. Coming out from the left bank were a host of little craft, not much more than a couple of planks tied together and propelled forward by two coolies, standing upright on them and using long oars.

Suddenly, for the first time since they had come to know him, Mr Chen looked genuinely worried. Smith caught his look and said urgently, 'What is it, Mr Chen?'

For once he was direct. 'Pirates – redbeards,' he answered.

Hurriedly Smith flung up his glasses. The light was almost gone, but the glasses helped. The men came into view. They looked rough and tough, some of them with very villainous faces indeed, but not one of them seemed armed.

'But they've got no weapons, if they're pirates,' Smith objected, lowering his glasses. 'A couple of them have knives, that's all, Mr Chen.'

'You see,' Mr Chen answered. 'There will be trouble.'

Smith was impressed by the Chinaman's seriousness. He acted at once. 'Stand by to repel boarders,' he yelled. 'Ginger, open fire if they get any closer.'

Ginger Kerrigan, manning the two Lewis guns on the monkey bridge, grinned hugely. 'Aye aye, sir,' he snapped back and wiped the raindrops from his wind-reddened face. He swung the ugly-looking machine guns round to face the men on the planks.

Suddenly, startlingly, a star shell hissed above the pinnace. In an instant it exploded, casting everything below in its ice-white, glowing light. Smith looked up, eyes narrowed against the glare. The shell could only have come from the Japanese gunboat. He felt an urgent sense of danger. Mr Chen was right. These civilians were dangerous and they were being aided by the Japs.

The star shell acted, it seemed as a signal. As one the paddlers were diving over the side of their primitive craft, heading for the shore in that funny kind of dogpaddle the Chinese used. Behind them their primitive floats continued towards the pinnace.

'What the devil's going on?' Smith snapped, as the swimmers struck out against the current. 'What do you make of that – jumping into the freezing water at–'

'Look, sir,' CPO Ferguson interrupted. 'Yon red things attached to them planks.'

McIntyre reacted first. 'They're mines!' he yelled. 'I'm sure.' He pulled out his Colt, cocked it and without appearing to aim, fired at the nearest of the red balls. His bullet struck home. Next instant the ball exploded in a spurt of ugly red flame, showering water all around it.

Ginger Kerrigan at the twin Lewis guns didn't wait for orders. He was too well trained and experienced for that. He pressed his trigger, swirling the ugly machine guns from left to right, hosing the river's surface with a hail of bullets. Ball after ball exploded, rocking the pinnace so that once it appeared its wireless mast almost touched the surface of the river. Wood and bits of rubber rained down everywhere as the crew hung on to stanchions as the craft heeled and recoiled under the shock of the multiple explosions.

Crack! Another star shell exploded directly above the pinnace. Instantly the little craft was bathed in its glowing icy-white light.

'The Japs again,' McIntyre said grimly as Ginger ceased firing, the danger over for the time being. He narrowed his eyes against the white incandescent glare. 'They're controlling this whole bloody business and you can bet who's behind it.'

'Who?' a worried Smith asked, as he eyed the opposite bank for further impending danger.

'Captain bloody Moto!' McIntyre spat out the name bitterly. 'He's behind the whole thing, the kidnapping, Mr Chen's redbeards, the whole damned lot.'

Smith nodded. 'I'spect you're right. But there's nothing much we can do about it. Look!'

At the controls CPO Ferguson exclaimed,

'The bloody bastards!' Automatically he signalled the engine room to slow down while there was still time, for stretched across the narrow gorge from one bank to the other, there was a stout chain.

Smith strained his eyes in the gloom, trying to assess the chain's strength. He knew instinctively that if they turned and tried to go back, the Japs would open fire on them. They had gone this far to aid their unknown attackers and they wouldn't back off now. He made a split-second decision. 'Chiefie, give her all the power you've got. We've got to burst through that chain or we're in bad trouble.'

CPO Ferguson looked for a moment as if he were going to protest. Hurriedly he spoke into the voice tube. The engines throbbed suddenly with full power. The pinnace surged forward. The deck beneath their feet quivered like a live thing. The graceful craft's sharp bow rose out of the water. Behind her she left a wake of wild white water flying to both sides. The chain loomed up ever larger. 'All ashore who's going ashore,' Dickie Bird whooped, carried away by the excitement and danger of it all.

'Hold on!' Smith yelled.

The prow of the pinnace struck the chain

at full speed. There was a great metallic twang. For a moment the craft seemed to stop. Then the chain snapped: its two halves hissed across the surface of the river like a huge steel whip. Then they were through, heading into the darkness at top speed, as the crew cheered and cheered. They'd done it again!

Chapter Two

Fu-zhou was strategically located on the Upper River, most of the ancient city being perched on a flat plateau over 1,000 foot high which, according to Mr Chen, could be reached only by a massive staircase cut into the rock. It was up there in a fortified three-storey *tingtze*, or a pavilion, that the warlord held his sway.

Now as the pinnace nosed its way towards the jetty, through the junks and light fishing sampans, the crew could see just how impregnable the place was. 'Yer need a regiment of marines to take that place,' Billy Bennett said, staring upwards, eyes narrowed against the rays of the sun.

'A whole bloody division to my way of thinking,' Ginger Kerrigan countered, 'and then some.'

Only CPO Ferguson wasn't impressed. 'A lot o' yellow chinks. Could nae fight their way out of a paperbag,' he growled. 'Why mon they stop fighting when it rains–' He halted suddenly. Five naked objects which had once been men came bobbing up and down in the water towards them. Their hands were bound with wire behind them and each body bore a crude sign around its chest. Where the heads had once been there was a great gory hole.

'Farmers who wouldn't pay tax,' Mr Chen translated the sign.

McIntyre spat over the side and said to Ferguson, 'Well, Jock, if they can't fight, they certainly know how to keep law and order – if that's what it is.' To which a shocked Ferguson could make no reply.

Smith had left Dickie in charge of the pinnace. Now with McIntyre and Mr Chen as interpreter, they pushed their way through the crowded streets to where the steps to the plateau above commenced. There were barefoot coolies, carrying live ducks on their heads. Haughty merchants in black gowns, with little boys shading their heads from the sun with paper parasols. Old men with wispy white beards carrying yellow singing-birds in cages which they listened to as they tottered by – and soldiers. There were soldiers everywhere in tattered uniforms, some barefoot, others wearing shoes made of straw, but all heavily armed and villainous-looking. More than once Smith thought they were going to be stopped and questioned by the soldiers who gave the impression they had never seen a white man before. But each time Mr Chen managed to fend them off by offering the soldier a small, almost worthless coin. These they took gratefully and went on their way, leaving the three of them to proceed.

However, at the entrance to the massive staircase they were stopped. This time the soldiers were smartly uniformed, wore proper boots and were washed and shaved. Again money changed hands. But this time the guards wanted notes not small coins. Mr Chen provided them and they could go on, but a soldier was posted to go with them. He did so climbing the stairs behind them, rifle pointed at their backs threateningly. 'I don't think we're particularly welcome,' Smith said, gasping a little and beginning to sweat with the heat and exertion.

'These war-lords have to guard their backs,' McIntyre said. 'There are a lot of other chaps who just like to take over and get their snouts in the trough.'

The war-lord was as McIntyre had described, small very fat and with the high-pitched squeak of a eunuch. But there was no doubt that he wasn't one. For as they approached his thronelike ornate seat raised on a dais at the end of the long hall, he was surrounded by armed soldiers and girls, lots of them. All of them were beautiful and dressed in sheer silk gowns with long slits up the sides so that it was clear that they were completely naked beneath the gowns. A couple of them were serenading him with mandolins, singing to the tune in squeaky voices that grated on Smith's ears. Still he couldn't take his eyes off them as the singers moved about, showing glimpses of their inner thighs, the nipples of their small breasts jutting through the thin tight material.

Mr Chen bowed low and said something. The war-lord clapped his soft pudgy hands. The music ceased immediately. The war-lord nodded to the tall stern officer standing next to the thronelike chair, pistol in hand, at the ready. Without taking his eyes off the newcomers for an instant, the officer reached his free hand into his pocket and pulling out a handful of gold coins, flung them on the floor.

The girls scrambled for them and Smith's eyes nearly popped out of his head as he caught glimpses of shaven, powdered pubes. They were really naked under the silk dresses.

The war-lord smiled, revealing a mouthful of gold teeth, but his dark cunning eyes did not light up. They remained wary as he assessed his three visitors. After a moment he crooked his finger at McIntyre who was in uniform and said something in Chinese.

At McIntyre's side Mr Chen whispered, without taking his eyes off the war-lord, for that would have been a sign of disrespect. 'The General asks you to approach and say what you want, Major.'

The big Canadian licked his lips and with Mr Chen at his side walked to the foot of the throne. He bowed and Smith could actually feel McIntyre's discomfort and embarrassment. He hated bowing to anyone. It went against his Canadian dislike of anyone in authority. Hurriedly McIntyre described their mission, while Mr Chen translated, bowing at regular intervals, as if he wished to show the war-lord just how much they respected him.

The war-lord listened attentively, rolling raw uncut gems between his fingers, the nails of which had been lacquered red, like some Greek might do with his worry beads. Mr Chen finished and, after a moment, the war-lord spoke in that strange high-pitched voice of his. 'He says,' Mr Chen translated in a whisper, 'he knows of the honourable missing Japanese princess. He asks, what do we want him to do about it.'

'Tell him,' McIntyre snapped, trying not to look at one of the girls, who was squatting in the corner, urinating loudly into a gold-painted jar, while at the same time whispering something to another girl, 'that we request his help in finding these pirates who have stolen her.'

Mr Chen translated and then after hearing the war-lord's reply, he said, 'The General knows where the redbeards are keeping the honourable princess, but he asks why he should help you.'

'Tell him it is to prevent a war between China and Japan,' Smith intervened hastily.

Mr Chen told him. The war-lord smiled softly, though still his dark eyes did not light up. He said something, his voice so low that

Mr Chen had to strain to hear him. Then he guffawed, his jowls trembling with the effort.

Mr Chen looked uncomfortable. It was the first time that Smith had seen him lose control of his emotions. Suddenly flustered, he stuttered, 'The General says it is no concern of his. War is his – how do you say – bread and butter.' Suddenly even his English, of which he was so proud seemed to desert him. 'He one bad Chink,' he concluded.

McIntyre looked at Smith and said out of the side of his mouth, 'I think we're going to have to bribe him.'

'Yes, you bribe me,' the war-lord said suddenly in passable English and grinned at them mischievously, showing that mouthful of gold teeth again.

Smith's mouth dropped open like that of some village idiot. The war-lord had out-smarted them all right. He'd understood what they had been saying all along. 'What ... what kind of bribe?' Smith stuttered, as the fat Chinese still continued to grin at them.

'I need an air force,' the war-lord replied. 'Every general must have an air force. You give.'

Again Smith was caught completely by surprise. *'An air force!'* he echoed foolishly, while Mr Chen hung his head, for he knew they had lost 'face'. 'But we can't give you an air force. I mean you'd need planes, pilots, mechanics – lots of money.'

The war-lord nodded at each point, as if in agreement before saying, 'One airplane for beginning. Little airplane good enough.' He beamed at the bemused Smith. 'You think.' He waved his hand, as if in dismissal. 'You have food, girls, drink.'

Mr Chen bowed and walking backwards, as if in the presence of royalty, moved away, followed by the other two, as the girls, shrieking and giggling, rushed forward to entertain their fat little master once more.

The tall officer with the drawn pistol caught up with them as they left the main entrance hall. He said something sharply to Mr Chen, pistol still clasped in his hand and gestured to a door on their right.

Mr Chen said, 'We are to be entertained in there till we make up our minds about the – er – air force.'

The tall officer didn't wait to see whether they had obeyed his command or not. He turned and rapped out an order. Half a dozen soldiers carrying rifles, with bayonets fixed, came doubling in and clicked to attention in front of the officer. He barked something and with their rifles held at waist-height, looking very grim and determined, they herded the three into the room. A moment later the door was firmly slammed to and locked behind them. 'Frig it,' McIntyre cursed, face red with fury. 'The shit's gone and taken us as his frigging prisoners.'

Sadly Mr Chen nodded his head. 'It seems to be that way, Major,' he agreed.

They sat down on the chairs which were grouped around the walls, each chair with a white enamel spitoon at its foot. These were at least clean, unlike the golden one which had rested on the dais next to the fat little war-lord. For a few minutes they lapsed into silence, each man wrapped in a cocoon of his own thoughts. For all three of them knew that no one could rescue them from this place, even if they had known that they were being held prisoner there.

Abruptly McIntyre broke the heavy silence with an angry, 'Let's promise him an airplane. But tell him it can't be delivered immediately until we get back to Shanghai. Then the fat bastard can go and take a running kick at himself.'

Mr Chen shook his head. 'I am afraid he would not accept that idea.'

'Yes,' Smith agreed. 'It's no tickee no washee with that feller. He'd hold us hostage here till the plane was delivered. No there's got to be some other way.'

Again the three of them fell silent.

'What about–' Smith began, but he never finished his question. For the door was flung open and half a dozen very pretty and very young Chinese girls came rushing in – all of them totally naked.

'Christ Almighty,' McIntyre exclaimed, *'enter the frigging dancing girls...'*

Chapter Three

A worried Dickie Bird flashed another look at his gold wrist-watch – the third time in the last ten minutes – and said to CPO Ferguson, 'Where in heaven's name have they got to, Chiefie? They should have been back ages ago now.'

CPO Ferguson stared up at the war-lord's home high above them on the plateau and said dourly, 'Nae trust a Chink, sir. Stab ye in the back as soon as look at ye, they would.'

Dickie Bird sighed, 'You're a real bundle of joy, Chiefie, that you are.'

'Just speaking ma mind, sir,' Ferguson said primly. Then he added, 'But I agree with ye, sir. Something must have gone wrong. Mr Smith and yon Colonial should have been back by now.'

Dickie Bird nodded and raising his glasses surveyed the 'pavilion' at the top of the great stone staircase yet again. Everything seemed in order. A group of soldiers were lounging at its head, smoking in a bored fashion. Some civilians were strolling in the ornamental gardens, followed by boys holding up parasols to ward off the rays of the late afternoon sun. The great door to the 'pavilion' was wide open and there was only a single sentry posted and he seemed to be dozing as he leaned against the wall. 'Nothing untowards there, Chiefie,' Dickie said and was just about to lower his glasses when he caught the winking light, coming from a ground floor window not far from the entrance. 'Hello, hello,' he said sharply.

'What is it, sir?' CPO Ferguson said eagerly.

'If I'm not mistaken, it's morse. Quick,

Chiefie, rustle up Bunts. He can read morse. I can't. Go on – leg it.'

CPO Ferguson 'legged it' as quickly as his old legs would carry him, while Dickie Bird flashed the lenses of his glasses up and down to convey that he had spotted the signal.

A moment later Bunts, the signaller, came running up to the deck, still clad in his underpants, muttering, 'Don't even have time for a quiet wank on this ship.'

Hurriedly Dickie handed him his binoculars. 'Window to the left of the main entrance, Bunts. Get it?'

Now Bunts was very professional. Standing there, looking a little absurd in his underpants, he pressed the glasses to his eyes and started to read the message. 'It's from Mr Smith, sir,' he said after a moment.

'What does he say?'

'Being held prisoner here, sir,' Bunts spelled out the words slowly. 'In no danger at the moment ... but could be ... try to get us out ASADP.'

'As soon as damn possible,' Dickie Bird said urgently. 'Here,' he took out the metal shaving mirror that he always kept in his breast pocket because he had once heard of another officer who had been saved from death when a German bullet had struck his metal shaving mirror and not his heart behind it. 'Send this.'

'Yessir,' Bunts snapped, and took the mirror.

'Nil desperandum—'

'What sir?'

'Never mind. Just send. "Don't despair. We'll come up with the doings toot sweet."'

Swiftly Bunts sent the message. High above them the light flickered a couple of times more and then stopped. 'Make it snappy,' Bunts read the message. 'Things are happening. Out.'

'Oh my sainted aunt!' Dickie Bird exclaimed. 'What the devil's going on up there?' He looked at CPO Ferguson aghast. The latter looked very solemn.

'Yon Chinks have some terrible tortures, sir,' he said dourly. 'They say the Chinks could make even a mummy talk.' He shook his grizzled head. 'Ay, yon three gentlemen'll be going through hell at this moment, I mind.'

With Oriental fatalism, Mr Chen had just let it happen. Now two naked girls 'attended' to him, as he had phrased it delicately, while he sipped rice wine, uttering subdued moans of pleasure in a very refined manner. McIntyre had resisted at first, yelling at the giggling naked whores, 'Get the hell out a here...' 'For Chrissake, get your hands off me, you damned little minx.' But their importunings had been too eager and he had succumbed. At this moment he was in the curtained-off couch at the far end of the room, striving mightily, making the springs creak noisily with his efforts.

It was while the other two had been occupied by the whores that Smith had sneaked to the window, drawing the heavy silken drapes behind him and had commenced signalling. Now he hid there, staring down at the gleaming white pinnace in the crowded harbour, wondering what Dickie Bird and Chiefie would do about attempting to free them. They were brave enough and they would try all right, but what could a handful of men like them do against the war-lord's army, which was many thousands of men strong?

He frowned, trying to ignore the noise coming from inside the room, while he attempted to work out a plan. He knew they didn't have much time. Once the girls were finished and they had been fed, the war-lord would want a decision; and somehow he felt the fat little man's demand for a plane in return for the location of the pirates was just a dodge. For reasons of his own the war-lord wanted the Jap princess killed and a war between China and Japan to start. In essence, the war-lord didn't want them to know where the pirates were hiding the princess.

Smith bit his bottom lip. Inside Mr Chen was moaning more loudly now. His pleasure was obviously so great while the two girls worked on him with their cunning lips and fingers, that he was even prepared to lose 'face' by moaning out loud. Smith forced himself not to listen. He had to come to some sort of decision, for he knew instinctively that the war-lord would not let them go. They might interfere with his plans for the princess. So he would either imprison them or have them quietly killed. That meant the crew of the *Swordfish* would have to be dealt with, too. Perhaps the fat swine with his high-pitched voice was already making plans to attack the pinnace. 'God,' he moaned to himself, 'what a mess!'

A thousand feet below, Dickie Bird spoke to the crew. He told them what had happened to three men in the pavilion and how he intended to do something to rescue them. 'First we must be prepared to sail immediately. That's your job, Chiefie and you'll mind the shop while I'm gone.'

CPO Ferguson looked as if he might object, then thought better of it.

'I shall take a boarding party with me,' the young officer went on. 'We'll take the Colts and the old cutlasses.'

'Cor ferk a duck!' Ginger Kerrigan exclaimed. 'Think we're back in Nelson's times. *Cutlasses!*'

'Best weapon there is if it comes to close quarters,' Dickie Bird said firmly. 'Now I'm sure we'll make the head of those stone stairs all right. But we'll probably have trouble with the entrance. A couple of rounds – very carefully placed – might do the trick, if we can get the six-pounder to reach that far.'

'Well within range, sir,' CPO Ferguson said firmly.

'Good. They'll give us the cover we need. But we'll dismantle one of the Lewis guns and take it with us. That'll be your job, Ginger.'

'Ay, ay, sir,' the latter replied promptly.

'May I make a suggestion, sir?' It was Billy Bennett who hadn't appeared to be listening so far.

'Suggest away. Well, go on, man.'

As always the fat sailor took his time, his brow wrinkled, as if he were given the matter a great deal of serious thought. 'Well, sir,' the fat sailor said finally while Dickie Bird fumed with impatience, 'we could really plaster them Chinks with the six-pounder if Mr Smith and the other gents were on the outside already. And seeing how Mr Smith was able to signal us, perhaps Bunts here,' he nodded to the signaller, 'could signal him what we're gonna do and that he should try to get outside that Chink place before the balloon goes up.'

Dickie Bird beamed with delight. 'My God, the Einstein of the lower deck!' he chortled enthusiastically. 'Billy, the next time we reach civilisation I'll stand you as many egg and chip dinners as your stomach can stand.'

'Can I have bangers as well, sir?' Billy said stoutly.

'Whole butcher shops full of 'em, Billy. Now Bunts signal this, will you...'

The girls had gone and the door had been locked on them once more. Soon, Smith reasoned, the food would be served and that would be the end of the war-lord's hospitality. The fun and games would commence then. McIntyre was doing up his flies, trying not to look the other two in the eye, while Mr Chen, obviously exhausted was fanning himself with a paper fan he had picked up somewhere or other. Smith could have laughed at the sight if the situation had not been so serious. 'Listen,' he said, keeping his voice low, 'I contacted the pinnace with that silver bowl.' He indicated a highly polished spitoon. 'They acknowledged. A minute ago while you two were still pigging yourselves, Dickie signalled they're going to try to get us out of this trap.'

McIntyre forgot his embarrassment. He flashed Smith a look. 'Boy, that's going to be tough,' he exclaimed. Mr Chen nodded his agreement, but said nothing.

'They're going to send up a boarding party and clobber the place with the six-pounder. But they want us out of it first, if we can manage it.'

'Sounds feasible. It'd take that fat bastard by surprise.' The initial look of new hope on his tough face vanished again. 'But how do we get out. We've got no weapons. No tools.'

'I think I may contradict there, gentlemen,' Mr Chen said quietly, stopping fanning himself. From his jacket pocket he produced the nail file with which Smith had often seen him file his nails of which he was inordinately proud. 'The key to most doors and windows, I am sure.'

Five minutes later they were outside, dropping out of the window which Mr Chen had opened quite easily with his nail file, just to see the long white shape slide into the harbour. And there was no mistaking those three crooked funnels of the craft. 'Christ,' McIntyre whispered softly, as they crouched there in the shrubbery, 'the Jap gunboat...'

Chapter Four

Dickie Bird gave the rickshaw drivers a handful of Chinese dollars. They bowed and were gone in a flash. They sensed something was wrong and they didn't want to be involved. Why were these white men so heavily armed? It was obvious they were looking for trouble.

Bird turned to Ginger Kerrigan who bore the Lewis gun over his right shoulder, wrapped in a piece of canvas. 'Stick close to me, Ginger,' he ordered. 'All right, off we go.'

They left the street, turned right and approached the bottom of the great stone stairway. The guards lounging there spotted them. For a while they didn't react. But slowly it began to dawn on them that there was something wrong. One of them, bigger than the rest, threw his cigarette away and held up his hand, as if to stop them.

Dickie Bird smiled winningly at him, but kept on going, saying in a stage whisper, 'Sorry, old bean, no can do.'

The big Chinese looked puzzled and then his bewilderment turned to apprehension. He started to unsling his rifle. Around him the other guards began to do the same. Still Dickie Bird kept on coming. The Chinese shouted something at him angrily. Dickie's inane smile broadened even more. The Chinese clicked off the safety on his rifle and looked threatening. Dickie's hand gripping the hilt of his cutlass was suddenly wet with sweat. This was it, he told himself. It was now or never. The Chinese started to aim his rifle, murder in his dark slanting eyes. He opened his mouth to shout something at the advancing white man. Dickie Bird didn't give him a chance. He lashed out with the cutlass. The Chinese screamed as his face was torn in two by the razor sharp blade. The rifle tumbled from his suddenly nerveless fingers. He went down on his knees moaning, and stared incredulously at the blood pouring over his upraised hands, as if he couldn't understand why this was happening to him.

Things moved swiftly now. Behind Ginger, his shipmate Billy Bennett raised the clumsy-looking brass signal pistol and pressed the trigger. In the same instant that the shore party closed in on the guards, laying about them with their cutlasses to left and right, the very red flare exploded in the afternoon sky above them. It was the signal that CPO Ferguson had been waiting for so tensely.

He ran to the edge of the bridge and bellowed to the waiting gun crew, 'Range one thousand feet ... fire at will!'

The three-man gun crew needed no urging. They knew that their shipmates had already run into trouble. They had to be quick if they were going to help them. The gun-layer had already elevated the gun to the target. Now opening his mouth automatically so that his eardrums wouldn't burst when he fired, he jerked back the firing handle. The six-pounder erupted in noise and flame. The shell shot from the muzzle as the empty case ejected from the smoking breech. The gun-layer followed it through the telescopic sight, as the gunner's mate thrust home another shell and slapped him on the shoulder to indicate that the six-pounder was re-loaded. Up on the heights Chinese were running everywhere in panicked confusion. Suddenly the shell exploded. Bodies flew through the air in spurts of ugly red flame. In the façade of the pavilion a great jagged hole appeared.

Dickie Ball waved his cutlass, now stained a bright red with Chinese blood. 'Come on, lads,' he cried above the racket, carried away by the crazy fury of battle. 'Up Guards and at 'em!'

The men ran after him, clambering up the steps, as a wild firing broke out from above. Ginger Kerrigan stopped. He whipped off the cover and, lodging the Lewis gun on the stone balustrade, pressed the trigger. The machine gun erupted in a wild fury. Tracer bullets sped upwards like a swarm of angry hornets. Wood and stone splinters rained down on the guards as they fell to the ground, some dead before they hit the ground. They clambered on.

Again the six inch cannon spoke. It slammed into the great door of the building.

Smith nudged McIntyre. It was time to go. In the confusion of the attack, he judged this was their opportunity. McIntyre nodded his agreement and tightened his grip on the chair leg which was his only weapon, though Mr Chen had produced a knife from somewhere or other. 'Let's go,' he cried.

They crept out of their hiding place in the shrubbery. A guard spotted them. He pointed his rifle at them and shouted something. Mr Chen reacted first. The knife flashed through the air. It caught the guard in the middle of his chest. Suddenly his tunic was stained a deep red. His knees started to give beneath him like those of a newly born foal. His rifle tumbled to the ground.

Smith darted forward and grabbed it. McIntyre gave the guard a brutal kick. He pitched forward on his face and then they were doubling to where Dickie Bird and the rest were fighting their way up the steps, with Billy Bennett, his face crimson, trying to keep up with them.

'Over here!' Smith cried and dodged as a slug slammed into the stonework next to his head. Automatically he raised his rifle and fired at the Chinese marksman. He went down clutching his shattered throat. *'Over here – Dickie!'*

Dickie Bird spotted them. He shouted something back but they couldn't catch his words. Instead they started to fight the way to the landing party, McIntyre laying about him with the chair leg in a wild apoplectic fury.

Even Mr Chen was showing himself a real fighter. But instead of using his hands, he was fighting with his feet, creating a devastating effect, with guards going down in front of him, clutching their ruined crotches into which he had slammed his foot.

Smith was first to reach Dickie's party. 'Good show, Dickie,' he gasped, wiping the blood from his forehead. 'Never been so glad to see you in my whole life.'

'Mutual, old bean,' Dickie said and fired over Smith's shoulder. A guard about to throw a grenade fell to the ground screaming, grenade still in his hand. Next moment it exploded, throwing him feet into the air, so that he splattered down, blood spurting from a dozen deadly wounds.

'Let's back off now, Dickie,' Smith yelled.

'Right-o. Can't be too soon for yours truly. Billy give the signal.'

Bennett was too winded to reply, but still he could act. He raised the bulbous flare pistol and pressed the trigger. A green flare exploded above their heads, colouring Billy's upturned face a sickly green hue.

CPO Ferguson below reacted immediately. 'All right, gun crew,' he bellowed, 'shrapnel!' He bent hurriedly to the voice tube. 'Stand by engine room. They're coming back now.'

At the six-pounder, the gun-layer waited till the shell was rammed into the smoking breech and the gunner's mate slapped his shoulder with a sharp *'in'* then he pulled the firing bar. The gun belched flame. 'Reload!' he yelled, watching for the impact of the first shell.

It exploded at the head of the great stone staircase. Shrapnel scythed lethally through the air. Chinese went down everywhere. Something like a yellow football came bouncing down from step to step. It was the head of one of the guards. The gun-layer fired again.

Now under the cover of the quick firer, Dickie Bird's party started to back off, knowing that Ferguson would keep up the barrage until they reached the street below. Then they would have to run for it.

On the Japanese gunboat, Captain Moto watched the fire fight through his glasses and cursed. He had thought that this time he would have finally been done with those damned round-eyes, the Englishmen. Instead they seemed to be escaping, as they had from the trap he had set for them two days before. He lowered his glasses and turned to Lieutenant-Commander Hashimoto, the captain of the gunboat. He did not bow or draw in his breath sharply as a sign of respect for a superior officer as he would normally have done. For he knew that Hashimoto did not approve of what was going on on the Yangtze. But then the Japanese Imperial Navy was a law unto itself. It would have no part of the plot which the Japanese Army's general staff had dreamed up last year. 'Commander,' Moto said coldly, 'we must do something to prevent the round-eyes from escaping yet again.'

Hashimoto, immaculate in white, his buttons gleaming gold, so that he could well have been taken for a British naval officer if he had not been so small and yellow-faced, looked coldly at the Intelligence Officer and asked, 'What do you expect me to do, Captain?'

'Stop them,' Moto answered bluntly.

'But that would be an act of war,' the

Commander protested hotly.

Moto shrugged carelessly. 'So what. We'll have to fight the white dogs in the end. If Japan,' he sucked in air reverently at the mention of the motherland, 'is to survive, we must defeat not only China, but also England and those American Yankees.'

Lieutenant-Commander Hashimoto was unimpressed. 'I take my orders from the Chief of the Imperial Navy,' he said coldly. 'I have given you accommodation on my ship and I have allowed you to have dealings with that unsavoury creature,' he pointed to the tall pock-marked Chinese with the pigtail standing at the bow watching the fire fight up on the staircase, 'and that's enough. I do not intend to engage a ship of a friendly power.'

Moto's dark eyes blazed behind his glasses. For a moment he looked as if he might strike the other man. Then, with an effort, he controlled himself. He said, 'I will report this conversation, Lieutenant-Commander. It will be held against you.'

Again Lt. Commander Hashimoto was unimpressed. 'So be it,' he said, and then, touching his hand to his cap in salute, 'Now I must be about my duties. We sail back to Shanghai in the hour.' He turned and without another word stalked off.

Moto stared at his skinny back, face contorted with rage. He'd make the swine pay for this in due course, he told himself. There were those among Hashimoto's officers who didn't share their captain's defeatist views. They would help him because they were patriots who were prepared to risk not only their careers but their very lives for the glorious cause of Nippon. 'Yes,' he whispered to himself, 'my revenge will be sweet, Commander Hashimoto.'

Now they were fighting their way down the street which led to the jetty and the pinnace. Bullets were whining off the walls on both sides of the little party. Up on the flat roofs civilians were throwing anything at hand at the retreating sailors. 'Christ, they'll be throwing the pisspots at us next!' Ginger Kerrigan gasped and fired one last burst from the Lewis gun at the roofs before, with a click, the gun went dead. The magazine was empty. Next moment a chamber pot exploded next to his feet, spraying him with urine. 'What did I tell yer, Billy. They'll be throwing pisspots next!'

Billy Bennett laughed in spite of the strain, and lashed out at a Chinese who had come out of a doorway, wielding a long spear. His cutlass went through the bamboo cane. The Chinese shouted something and stared at his useless weapon, as if he couldn't understand what had happened. Billy Bennett didn't give him time to consider very long. He lashed out again with his cutlass and the man reeled back, a gaping gory hole where his nose had just been.

Now the pinnace came into sight. CPO Ferguson had lined up along the deck the few men he had available, all armed with rifles. He himself was manning the other Lewis gun. Below him the engines were already throbbing and the pinnace quivered like a highly strung, thoroughbred dog impatient to be let off the leash. *'Run for it!'* he bellowed above the angry snap-and-crackle of the fire fight. *'Quick!'*

'You heard Chiefie, lads,' Dickie Bird yelled, 'break off the engagement and run for it!'

The men reacted as one. They stopped their attempts to fight off the advancing Chinese and ran for the pinnace. CPO Ferguson didn't hesitate. Jutting out his skinny jaw, he pressed the trigger of the Lewis gun. Tracer sped lethally over the heads of the running men to where the Chinese, yelling in triumph, started to come out of the doorways in pursuit. Abruptly the Chinese were galvanised into crazy action like puppets in the hands of a puppeteer suddenly gone mad. Jerking and screaming, twisted right round under the impact of that cruel fire, they fell in their dozens and then in scores. In an instant the street was transformed into a path of death. Everywhere there were dead and dying writhing pitifully in their last agonies. The Chinese had been beaten.

Fifteen minutes later the pinnace was sailing swiftly past the anchored Japanese gunboat, but not too swiftly for the officers on the bridge to spot an angry-looking Captain Moto and the villainous Chinese with the pigtail standing next to him.

McIntyre still bleeding from a cut on the forehead gasped with surprise. Next to him, Mr Chen said simply, 'Redbeard.' It was a pirate chief who had captured the Japanese princess.

Chapter Five

'*Here she comes,*' Smith said softly, as the Japanese gunboat turned the bend in the Yangtze. They had camouflaged the pinnace well. They had sailed her into a narrow inlet on the wooded left bank of the great river. Immediately the crew had set to work lopping off branches and draping them around the little craft until after half an hour later, Dickie Bird, surveying the pinnace from fifty feet away, confirmed that she wouldn't be visible to any casual observer from the Yangtze.

Now the crew watched tensely as the Japanese gunboat started to slacken speed, as if she might even anchor some two hundred yards or so away.

'What do you make of it, Smith?' McIntyre asked urgently.

'I think they're going to get rid of Mr Chen's red beard,' Smith answered in a whisper. 'I'm sure they know we've seen them with him, so they might have concluded we've signalled RAY what we've spotted. And whatever they're damn well up to, they don't want to be compromised by being seen with the Chink – excuse me, Mr Chen – the Chinese pirate…'

McIntyre nodded his understanding. 'Yeah, you're right, Smith. But what damned Sam Hill are they going to do with that Jap princess?' He frowned with frustrated anger.

Smith didn't answer. He concentrated on the Japanese gunboat, which had now come to a stop in the middle of the river. He would have dearly loved to have surveyed it through his binoculars, but dare not; the glint of the lenses in the evening sun might have given their position away.

Minutes ticked by tensely. Then they spotted a familiar figure. It was Captain Moto. In his hand he was carrying a small leather attaché case. He strode to the rail, lugging his overlong samurai sword behind him in an absurd fashion and stared at the opposite bank. After a while he was joined by the redbeard. They spoke together. Then with a slight bow he handed the attaché case to the pirate.

Smith thought he saw the red beard smile, as he tested the weight of the case, lifting it up and down a couple of times.

'What do you make of that?' Dickie Bird asked in a taut whisper.

'Money,' McIntyre answered. 'I'm sure that's the dough they're bribing the Chinese with.'

Behind, Mr Chen nodded and said, 'Yes, surely a farewell gift. Look.' He pointed to the opposite bank. A small junk, appearing from nowhere, was beginning to head for the stationary gunboat. 'More redbeards.'

'You're right,' Smith said eagerly. 'This is surely the parting of the way and we're here at the parting.' His face lit up. 'Now at last, we're on to them.'

'Yes,' McIntyre snorted. 'We've got the buggers.' He watched as the helmsman steered the junk towards the gunboat, her deck filled with heavily-armed men, some of whom had great gleaming belts of cartridges around their waists and shoulders. 'Now, as soon as that Nip gunboat takes off, we'll be after them.'

Smith nodded, but said nothing. His mind was racing. He was sure that Captain Moto would want to see the junk safely underway before the gunboat sailed again. But how long would the Japs stay there in midstream? He hoped to heaven not too long. Otherwise they'd lose the scent.

On the deck of the gunboat Lt. Commander Hashimoto looked scornfully at the Chinese and Captain Moto. He knew the latter would regard it as an act of provocation, but he didn't give a damn. Once the yellow dog was overside he would order the decks swabbed. That would remove all trace of the villain.

Captain Moto deigned to take the Chinese pirate's hand. The latter gave him a crooked smile, touched the case containing the money, and said softly in Japanese, 'Your orders will be carried out to the letter, Captain Moto.'

The latter touched his white gloved hand to his cap in salute and deftly the Chinese started to descend the ladder to the waiting junk. Moto turned and stared coldly through his thick glasses at the captain. 'I suggest we wait here, Commander, till the Junk is out of sight. A little bit of protection.'

Lt. Commander Hashimoto stared back equally coldly and said, iron in his voice, 'I give the orders on this ship, Captain Moto. Not you.'

'But you must understand–'

'I understand what I want to understand.

No more,' the commander interrupted him sharply. 'Now I want to get underway.' He turned and shouted to his Number One, 'Lieutenant, get the swabbing party onto this deck. It's filthy. Clean it down at once.' He flung a look over his shoulder at an angry Moto. 'The stink is unbearable.' Minutes later the gunboat was chugging down the Yangtze once more, heading away from Shanghai.

'Wow,' McIntyre breathed out hard. 'This is it.'

'Yes,' Smith agreed. 'It was bit nip-and-tuck. All right, Chiefie, let's get underway.'

'What about all these bits o' trees, messing up my boat,' Ferguson protested.

'No time for that,' Smith answered. '*Your* boat will have to stay messed up. We've got to get after those redbeards.'

Now the sun had disappeared behind the cliff. Dark shadows swept down the Yangtze. The junk had a headstart and it carried no riding lights. Smith knew they daren't get too close or the Chinese would spot them. On the other hand, if they stayed too far behind, the junk could disappear into one of the many side-arms which ran into the Yangtze on this section of the great river. He sucked his lips with a worried frown on his face till CPO Ferguson said, 'Dinna fash yersen, sir. We'll keep tags on you Chink bugger, ye can be certain o' that.'

But CPO Ferguson proved to be wrong. They allowed the junk to sail around the next bend of the river at a section where sheer white cliffs towered up on both sides to the darkening sky. But when the pinnace did the same, the junk had vanished. 'Holy cow,' Dickie Bird exclaimed, 'she's gone!'

'But she can't have,' Smith objected. 'She couldn't have made it down that stretch – why it must be at least four hundred yards or more – and vanish just like that.' He clicked his thumb and forefinger together sharply.

'Shall I take her about, sir?' CPO Ferguson asked. 'You dinna ken, sir. She might have gone into hiding. There's plenty of trees and the like on yon bank.'

'Do that,' Smith said swiftly. 'Before the damned light goes altogether.'

Expertly Ferguson swung the pinnace round. At a snail's pace they began to crawl back the way they had come, the lookouts straining their eyes in the growing gloom in an attempt to stop the vanished junk.

But they were out of luck. There was no sign of the pirate craft.

In despair, knowing that they might be

giving their own position away by doing so, Smith ordered, 'Dickie, fire a flare. Let's have a proper look-see.'

Bird reached for the flare pistol clipped to the bulkhead and clicked off the safety. 'Are you ready everybody?' he called, as he raised the pistol above his head. Next instant he pressed the trigger.

Plop! A sharp crack and the flare exploded above the bank in a blaze of brilliant white light which had them blinking their eyes for a moment. Then they spotted it. A narrow stretch of water, leading from the Yangtze and disappearing into the side of the cliff. It was one of many they had spotted over the recent days.

'That must be it,' Smith said, as CPO Ferguson turned the pinnace in that direction and up front the sailor with the leaded line started to call out the depths as they came ever closer to the sidearm. 'They know the river like the back of their hand. They must have used that side-arm many a time, banking on the fact that it's so shallow, no gunboat could follow them up it.'

'Exactly,' Dickie Bird cried, as the man at the bow called out the fathoms. 'But they hadn't reckoned on the draught of this little beauty.'

'Thank God for it,' Smith agreed, as they nosed their way into the channel, with the pinnace's screw barely clearing the bottom.

'Stand by the gun crew,' Smith ordered as they began to sail deeper into the side-arm, both sides of which were covered with thick vegetation: an ideal place for an ambush, he told himself.

Hurriedly the three-man gun crew manned the sixpounder, while Ginger Kerrigan swung himself behind the twin Lewis guns once more.

Now they tensed in almost absolute darkness, the only sound the soft purr of their engines, as Smith peered through the night glasses in an attempt to find the missing junk. Time passed slowly. Each man was wrapped up in a cocoon of his thoughts and fears. If they were caught now, they wouldn't stand a chance. There would be no escaping like they had done from the warlord's palace. All of them knew that.

Suddenly Smith broke the silence with a hissed, 'There she is. Stop engines, Chiefie.'

The Thorneycrofts stopped almost immediately and as the pinnace drifted forward slowly, they could see the junk now, as it was tied up to a rough wooden jetty adjacent to a group of tumble-down huts, lit by flickering candles and storm lanterns. Hastily CPO Ferguson steered the silent pinnace into a little inlet some hundred yards or so away from the pirate camp.

Smith whispered, 'Quick thinking, Chiefie.' Then he turned to McIntyre and Dickie Bird, voice urgent, face set, 'We go in this very night.'

'Yep,' McIntyre agreed. 'My guess is that Captain Moto paid the big chap to bump off the princess. Perhaps they won't do it tonight ... no, I don't think they will. They'll do it tomorrow in daylight because they'll want to take a photograph of her to send to the authorities. They always send photos of their kidnap victims when they demand a ransom. Yes, it'll be tomorrow morning. Then they'll quit the camp toot sweet.'

Smith absorbed the information for a moment before saying, 'We must plan our attack carefully. We don't want her getting hurt. That's vital. We must get her out of that place in one piece. Because if we don't, China and Japan might well be at war within the next few days.' He looked significantly at the others in gloom and added, 'There must be no slip-ups, because if we mess this one up, there's no calculating where it all may end.'

Chapter Six

Outside the hut in the velvet gloom, her captors were drinking what they called 'Horse-tit wine', *kumess*, sour mare's milk fermented, and talking drunkenly. The wine had loosened their tongues and they were talking about her in the manner of the simple peasants they had once been. They were wondering whether she was built like their women and whether Japanese women had hair between their legs. They had heard that foreign women liked their breasts kissed and nipples sucked. But that was for children. Chinese women wanted the backs of their necks kissed. That was very exciting.

She sat there on the mat, listening and worrying. She had not told them she understood some Chinese when they had kidnapped her. Now her knowledge of their language had improved and she was using it to try to learn what they intended for her, bad or good.

The princess was no longer the fashionably dressed Japanese woman who had stepped off the boat in Shanghai to be so rudely abducted. The lacquered coiffeur had gone as had the white-powdered face. In place of her expensive elegant kimono, she now wore a simple black cotton peasant suit of smock and trousers. But they had not treated her badly otherwise. They had fed her well with the same plain rice diet they ate themselves. They had not attempted to rape or touch, though once or twice she had caught some of the younger ones spying on her when she had been making water. They, like those outside now, seemed to think that foreign women would be built differently, hence the spying.

All the same she knew that they would profit from her kidnapping one way or another. Was she being held for ransom? Was that it? But if so, why hadn't the General, her husband-to-be, paid the ransom by now? Surely he had had time enough to do so. Was there something else behind it all, she wondered.

An hour before, she had seen the return of their leader, the one with the pigtail, through a gap in the wood and straw that the hut was constructed of. He had been very excited and they had become excited too when he had slapped the case he had been carrying and said something, which she had not understood, in Chinese. Since then most of her guards had been drinking the fermented mare's milk, getting progressively more drunk.

She sat back on her heels and thought. She was not afraid. She had never been afraid of anything because she had been taught that discipline overcame fear. Besides she would lose 'face' if she ever showed fear. All the same she was apprehensive. The arrival back of the pigtailed leader had changed the atmosphere of the little camp on the river. Up to now her guards had been stern and sober. Why were they getting drunk this night? Were they celebrating something, and if they were, had it anything to do with her?

She bit her bottom lip. She knew she could escape, if she wanted to, especially now when they were getting drunk. But where was she? Where would the nearest friendly people be? For all she knew she was in some remote wilderness, for they had kept her blindfolded most of the time that the junk had reached this place. And she was fairly sure it was remote, for once she had heard the baying of a tiger or something like it and not once had she heard the sounds of domestic animals, the bells of goats or the quacking of ducks, which the Chinese so dearly loved to eat. At the beginning she had forced herself to wake at dawn, resourceful woman that she was, and listen for the sound of a cock crowing. That would have indicated a village nearby. But there had been nothing, just the muted hush of the dawn wind in the trees.

Outside the chatter of the drunken guards was dying away. Perhaps they had run out of drink, she told herself. Or perhaps they were just sleepy. She yawned and thought she ought to get some sleep herself. Sleep would blot out the uncertainty for a few hours at least. Yet when she lay on the straw pallet which was her bed, she couldn't sleep. Something compelled her to stay awake. She did not know what exactly, but she simply couldn't drop off, try as she may.

Now the guards had ceased talking altogether. She could hear some of them snoring in a drunken sleep. Silence descended upon the remote little camp, broken only by the sound of the wind in the trees. Still the princess could not sleep.

'Dickie,' Smith hissed, 'you go in on the left flank. Major McIntyre, you'll take the right if you would. Chiefie and I will go straight into the hamlet.'

McIntyre, the veteran of the trenches, eyed the dark stark outline of the handful of crude huts. A sickle moon had risen and was bathing the area in a spectral cold light. He felt the old mixture of tension and excitement surge through him. It was just like going on a show, out to raid the German positions for a prisoner for identification. The adrenalin had always flown faster at such times. He whispered, 'The trick is to make it snappy. Hit 'em fast and furious. Don't give 'em a chance to recover. Once you get bogged down in house-to-house fighting you're sunk. Got it?'

'Got it,' Smith answered with a faint grin. McInytre was taking over, but then he was the expert. They were just inexperienced sailor-boys to him.

'All right,' Smith raised his hand to see the luminous dial of his wrist-watch, 'it's twenty-four hundred hours. Let's c–'

'Circumcise our watches,' Dickie Bird beat him to it cheekily.

'Right then, off we go,' Smith ordered and, nodding to CPO Ferguson, who was carrying a wicked-looking cosh in addition to his Colt and cutlass, set off down the little trail which led to the huts. To left and right, the others melted into the trees.

The princess woke with a start. Something was moving in the trees to the rear of the little camp. For a moment she felt afraid. Was it the tiger, she had heard before? She had read that when tigers were hungry, they would attack a human being. Then she reasoned it couldn't be. A tiger would be frightened off by the fire still burning in the centre of the camp, which two of the drunken guards sprawled beside, their duties neglected, snoring loudly but with rifles at their sides. But what was it? What could be moving so stealthily about at this time of night?

She sat up and ran her hands through her hair, feeling a growing sense of excitement. Was it a rescue party? Could that be possible? But if it were a rescue party and her guards were alerted, what would they do? Would they try to kill her before she could be saved? She considered the problem, while the sounds, faint as they were, grew closer. She decided the guards would try and murder her before they fled. Swiftly she looked around the little straw-roofed hut for some weapon to defend herself until the rescue took place. But there was nothing, save the tin in which she made water and the spitoon with which they had provided her, though she didn't spit, as the Chinese seemed to be doing all the time.

She bit her bottom lip, wondering what she should do. Then she had it. Swiftly, silently, she reached up, standing on her toes, and started pulling the straw of the roof apart. Cooler air came in and she could see the pale glow of the moon. Suddenly she felt renewed hope. She was going to be saved. She worked more rapidly, knowing that time was running out. She had to disappear – and disappear soon.

Smith paused. Behind him Ferguson gripped his cosh more tightly. They were at the outskirts to the hamlet. All was silent, save for the snores of those in the huts. In the centre of the camp a dying fire cast a ruddy glow over the dirt square. Smith flashed a look at the green-glowing dial of his watch. He nodded. He judged that the other two parties on the flanks would be in position now. But where were they keeping the Japanese princess?

He stroked his jaw as he considered and, as if he could read the young officer's mind, Ferguson hissed, 'It's logical, sir. In the centre o' yon place.'

'You're right, Chiefie,' Smith whispered

back. 'Come on. Let's see if we can find her before the ruddy balloon goes up.'

Cautiously, they stole forward. In the coals of the dying fire, they could see the two sleeping guards, sprawled out with their rifles at their side. 'Leave 'em to me, sir,' Ferguson whispered. On tiptoe he advanced across the opening. Suddenly he stopped dead. A figure was coming out of one of the huts. The Chinese was clad only in a vest. He advanced a few paces and then, eyes almost closed with sleep, began to urinate on the ground.

The noise made one of the guards stir. He muttered something and then, turning over, went back to sleep. Ferguson nodded his approval.

Scratching his naked yellow rump, the Chinese went back into the hut once more. Ferguson waited another minute then he went in, cosh raised. He halted by the first, judged where to hit him and brought the leaded cosh down smartly. The guard gave a little grunt. His head lolled even further. 'Now you'll sleep nice and sound,' Ferguson whispered to himself and turned to the second man. Suddenly the latter stirred and sat up abruptly. His eyes opened. In the lurid glow cast by the dying embers he saw the old white man with the club in his hand standing over him. He recoiled in horror, as if he were seeing a ghost. Ferguson struck – and missed. 'Blast it,' he cursed and raised his club once more.

The guard didn't give him chance to strike again. Abandoning his rifle, he was on his feet, running for the nearest hut, crying out loudly in absolute fear.

'That's torn it,' Smith cursed.

It had. In a flash the camp was in an uproar. Chinese, mostly half naked, burst from the huts. There were shouts, cries of alarm and rage. A shot rang out. Then several more. On both flanks the two parties converged on the camp. In the lead of his party, McIntyre was snapping off shots to left and right, Chinese yelled and fell. Others attempted to run for the cover of the trees. McIntyre showed no mercy, but fired at their running backs. They went down too, yelling with pain.

Followed by Ferguson, Smith, pistol in his hand, cutlass ready in the other, ran into the centre of the hutted camp yelling, 'Surrender surrender,' knowing that the Chinese wouldn't understand, but that their captive might. A Chinese charged at him, brandishing a sword. Smith raised his pistol, fired and missed. Next moment the Chinese slashed the blade at him. Metal struck metal as a desperate Smith parried the blow with his own cutlass. Exerting all his strength, face purple with the effort, Smith thrust the Chinese back, as they had been taught to do in Dartmouth before the war. Next instant he had thrust his own weapon up and down, slashing the Chinese across the face. The man screamed shrilly. The sword tumbled from his fingers. Next moment he went down on his knees. Smith slammed the pommel into his bloody face and, springing over his falling body, ran on.

Now the camp was a chaotic mess of men struggling together at close quarters. Steel clashed against steel. Shots rang out. Men cursed and swore, as they had swayed back and forth in hand-to-hand fighting; gouging, slashing, cutting. No quarter was given or expected. But the pirates had been caught by surprise and the attackers were gaining the upperhand. In the lead of his party, McIntyre, the veteran of the trenches, knew that the heart would go out of the defenders if he could nail their leader, the Chinese with the pigtail. He had to find that Chink.

Smith and Ferguson, brushing aside whatever opposition they encountered, concentrated on finding the princess. Smith was sure she had to be in one of the huts, now they were emptied of Chinese. But which one?

The man with the pigtail was intent on the same mission. Once the execution had been carried out, Captain Moto had promised a further payment. Now he was desperate to find the princess before these foreign devils did. He knew the Japanese. They were a hard people. They wouldn't give him the gold unless he brought concrete evidence that the princess was dead. Leaving his followers to defend themselves against this surprise attack the best they could, he dodged in and out of the mêlée to the hut where they kept the princess imprisoned.

'Come,' he ordered in Japanese. 'I will save–' He stopped short – she was gone. There was no one in the hut. For a moment his brain stopped working. But how could she have got away? Suddenly it dawned on him. A silver light was reflected on the dirt floor. It was coming from a hole in the straw roof through which the moonlight shone. Despite the danger, a brief smile crossed his evil, pock-marked face. She was hiding up on the roof. Now he had her. He reached up and raised himself.

In a moment he'd slice off her head, the evidence Moto would require, and be gone. He grinned at the thought of the reward in gold to come, and pulled himself through the hole.

Chapter Seven

'Empty!' Smith cursed as he ran into the entrance of yet another hut and peered into the gloom to find nothing.

'Dinna fash yersen, sir,' Ferguson consoled. 'We'll find yon Jap lassie soon.' He ducked as a bullet slammed into the bamboo wall of the hut and showered them with splinters. 'Ye cheeky bugger, firing at a chief petty officer in King George's navy,' Ferguson snorted and fired back.

There was a yelp of pain and a half-naked Chinese slammed to the ground and lay still.

'Come on,' Smith cried above the angry snap-and-crackle of the fire fight. They ran to the next hut and it was then that they heard the shrill scream of a woman. 'It's her!' Smith cried in triumph. He burst into the hut. It was empty. 'What the hell—' he said, standing there bewildered, chest heaving.

The woman screamed again and Smith could hear the sound now of the struggle overhead. He saw the hole in the roof and snapped, 'Come on, Chiefie, outside!'

They sped out and stared up at the roof. Two figures were outlined there in the cold light of the moon: an ugly-looking Chinese, his sword upraised, and a terrified woman, her smock torn to reveal her breasts, hands held in front of her protectively.

The Chinese shouted something and grabbed her black hair. She shrieked as he tugged it to force her head backwards. His sword gleamed in the light as the muscles of his naked right arm hardened for the stroke. Instinctively Smith knew what he was going to do. He was about to slice off her head.

Praying he wouldn't miss, Smith aimed and fired in the same instant. The big man grunted hard and deep. His body suddenly went rigid. He froze in the same position – and tugging the woman's hair, sword upraised – as if for eternity. For a moment Smith thought he had missed and he took first pressure on the trigger of his pistol once again. Suddenly, startlingly, however, the Chinaman's knees started to crumple. He released his grip on the terrified girl's hair. His sword arm started to tremble violently, as if he were fighting back, determined not to be deprived of his victim.

It was thus that Dickie Bird came upon them, fighting his way through the mêlée – the dying Chinese and the terrified half-naked girl standing above him on the roof. 'Oh, I say,' he exclaimed, 'what a performance!'

Suddenly the girl slammed her shoe into the big Chinaman's knee. He yelled. The sword fell from his hand. Slowly, very slowly, he stumbled backwards, as the girl overcame her fear and kicked him again – hard. The Chinaman muttered something and then he was over the side of the roof, slamming to the ground at Dickie Bird's feet and gold coins rolling from his pockets as he lay there spread-eagled, dying.

Here and there the sailors bound up their wounds and cuts. Others contented themselves simply with leaning against walls and staring at the Chinese dead, as if an invisible tap had been opened allowing all energy to drain from them.

McIntyre, however, seemed as full of

beans as ever. Together with Mr Chen he rounded up the survivors of the redbeards and questioned them through the latter. The prisoners were surly and reluctant, but the big Canadian had no time to waste and he wanted answers to his questions – and fast. Every time one of the prisoners hesitated, he clapped his hand to his pistol holster significantly and then they talked.

While McIntyre cross-examined the prisoners and Smith organized the crew for the return to the pinnace, Dickie Bird attended to Princess Sadako, or 'Sadie', as she told him he should call her. Swiftly she had slipped into the new smock he had found her, while he looked the other way and told her what their mission was. Now he listened while she told him in her excellent American English how she had been kidnapped and what had happened afterwards. 'I guess, I didn't expect the worse,' she explained, while he took in her beautiful face and excellent figure. 'But somehow at the back of my mind when the ransom didn't come from the General,' she shrugged, 'well, I thought anything could happen.' She looked at him winningly and he felt his heart miss a beat.

'I think it might,' Dickie said quietly. 'But

now you're safe. With me – er,' he corrected himself hastily, 'with *us*.' Dickie Bird was glad the light was so poor for he felt himself blushing. 'Good grief, Dickie, old bean,' he said to himself, 'I really think you're smitten. Oh, my sainted aunt!'

Smith approached. 'Princess we're going–'

'*Sadie*,' she corrected him with another of her delightful smiles.

'All right then, Sadie, we're going back to our boat. Lieutenant Bird here will see you're all right. Once aboard, we'll get you back to Shanghai as soon as we can. It'll be pretty tight on board, but we'll manage.'

'Sure we will,' she answered. 'It's gonna be swell to get out of this dump. I can tell you.'

Five minutes later, after breaking the firing pins of the Chinese soldiers rifles and throwing the bolts into the bushes, the party set off again for the pinnace, leaving their former prisoners squatting on their haunches staring after them – bitter, impotent anger in their eyes.

They moved quickly, for as McIntyre had rasped just before they left, 'I don't think we're out of the woods yet. From what I learned from those guys this is a really big operation. I don't think Captain Moto and the rest of them,' he didn't specify who the 'rest' were, 'are going to let us off the hook that easily.'

Smith would have dearly loved to have asked McIntyre what the operation was but there was no time for that, so he concentrated on getting the party back to the pinnace safely.

The Princess caught the name Moto. Now she said to Dickie at her side, 'Captain Moto is my fiancé's Intelligence Officer. What has he got to do with all this?'

''Fraid, I don't really know, Sadie. But we do know he was mixed up with those pirate chappies who kidnapped you.'

She gasped with shock. 'And Captain Moto,' she said slowly and thoughtfully, 'would do nothing without the permission of the General. So that must mean that my fiancé – the General – is mixed up in it, too.'

'You might be right,' Dickie answered, now only half listening to her, for suddenly he thought he heard noises some way off, like those of horses chomping at their bits and snorting. Instinctively he reached for his Colt. Abruptly there was tension in the air again.

Smith, who was at the head of the party, dropped back to where Dickie was in the column's middle and said in a low tone,

'Did you hear it?' Dickie nodded sombrely.

'Can't be peasants,' Smith said. 'They wouldn't be about at this time of the night. Besides peasants don't have horses.' He looked worried. 'Keep your eyes skinned, Dickie.'

'Like the proverbial tinned tomato, old chap,' Dickie answered with an attempt at light-heartedness, though his eyes remained worried.

Sadie said, 'Who can it be?'

'Search me, Sadie. But anyone out at this time of night in China on horseback can't be up to any good in my humble opinion.'

Suddenly she clutched his arm. 'You'll look after me, Dickie, won't you?' It was the first time she had used his first name and despite the tension he felt a thrill. 'I couldn't stand being cooped up again.'

'Of course, of course,' he reassured her and pressed her hand.

They moved on, every man on the alert now, with McIntyre bringing up the rear, throwing frequent glances behind him. But always there was nothing there. 'Soon be seeing the pinnace,' Smith at the head of the column called reassuringly. 'Just round the bend, chaps.'

'I hope so,' Billy Bennett grumbled to his

shipmate, Ginger Kerrigan. 'My guts are doing backflips. I'm that starved, I could eat a horse.'

'With the belly you've got, you look as if you have already scoffed one,' Ginger said unfeelingly. 'You're allus thinking of grub – Me, I'm a beaver man mesen.'

'It takes grub to put lead in yer pencil,' Billy answered. 'You've got to eat plenty o' chips and things, if you want to get yer pecker–' He stopped short. Up front Smith had come to a halt. The column did the same.

'What's up, d'yer think, Billy?' Ginger asked in sudden alarm. 'Not more frigging Chinks?'

'How should I know,' his shipmate snorted. 'I ain't bleeding Jesus Christ, yer know...'

CPO Ferguson pushed forward to where the young officer was standing. 'Trouble sir?' he asked.

Smith didn't speak for a moment and, peering over his shoulder, CPO Ferguson could see in the cold light of the moon what Smith was staring at. 'Hell's bells!' he gasped. 'Somebody's been at the radio mast.'

Someone had. The mast had been broken

half-way down. The top had been thrown into the water so that now only the stump remained, wreathed in broken wires.

'What do ye make of it, sir?' Ferguson asked.

'I don't really know,' Smith answered hesitantly, his young face grim. 'All I know is we've got a couple of hundred miles of the Yangtze in front of us and if there's trouble, we haven't got a hope in hell of summoning up help from RAY in Shanghai. We're on our own, Chiefie.' His voice rose. 'All right, there's no use moaning about it. Let's get aboard and underway. I don't like this place one bit.'

'Ay,' Ferguson agreed, shivering a little, as if he suddenly had become cold. 'Nae use greeting over spilled milk, sir.'

Ten minutes later they were on their way once more, chugging down the inlet to the great river beyond. But instead of the usual jolly mood after a successful operation, the crew were sombre and apprehensive, eyeing the shadows to both sides as they slid by, with tension written all over their faces. For they knew now someone – the someone who had wrecked the radio mast – was out there, watching them...

Captain K'uang waited till the little craft had disappeared around the bend. He would have dearly loved to attack the foreign Imperialists himself. But he knew his handful of cavalrymen wouldn't have stood much chance against the enemy's twin machine guns and cannon. But he had done his part, for a start. They were out of touch with their fellow Imperialists. Now he would report to Comrade Borodin what he had done. Thereafter it would be up to the Squad of Sudden Death to deal with them. He tugged at the bit of his horse and turned it round. 'Come comrades,' he ordered. 'The redbeards have failed, but we won't.'

There was a murmur of agreement among his men. Now they would raid the nearest village, take their food and rape their women. It would be their reward for the weeks they had spent on reconnaissance behind enemy lines. Perhaps there might be some rich merchant too, with gold coins hidden below the floor of his house. Even in the great classless society soon to come, gold would retain its value.

But Captain K'uang dreamed another dream. Of China, this a land of fields, woods, lush pastures criss-crossed with placid canals, a land of prosperous peasants with healthy bullocks, where everyone had plenty of rice and roast pork – and where the barbarians were safely behind the Great Wall and the round-eyed foreign devils were only a distant rumour. The dream warmed him despite the chill of the night, and he smiled. Soon there'd be a war and then their time would come. He started to hum to himself quite happily.

Chapter Eight

'We Japanese are a very curious people,' Sadie lectured them as they lounged in the afternoon sunshine on the forrard deck. 'On the surface we seem well ordered, calm and disciplined. In reality we are very different.' She looked around her little audience of Smith, Bird, McIntyre and Mr Chen. Dickie Bird smiled back at her winningly.

'In Japan a belch is a compliment. In Japan an officer sentenced to death is shot through a curtain because it is thought inconceivable that a private should see that he is actually shooting a person of higher rank. A cup of tea has to be drunk in exactly three and a half gulps. No more, no less.' She smiled at the looks on their faces.

'In Japan,' she continued, 'gardens are protected from the north west with shrubbery because it is supposed that it is from that direction the evil spirits will enter your house.' She shrugged slightly. 'We are not at all what foreigners think we are.'

Mr Chen, as always very polite, seemed to be listening. In fact, his mind was on the great river down which they sailed. How broad and majestic it was, he told himself. It was bad and it was good. In times of flood it killed land and people, leaving behind it famines that could bring death to millions. But it was a symbol of strength, China's strength. A great trading route, older and more powerful than the Old Silk Road. But although there were Chinese fishing sampans and junks on it this glassy afternoon, it was really in the hands of the foreign devils, the round-eyes.

These people he was with were his friends, but still they were of those foreigners who controlled the river, ran its trade and made the huge profits, while China slipped ever deeper into poverty. It wasn't right, he told himself. But he would help them. He had to!

'So,' the Princess was saying, 'on the surface everything about us Japanese seems calm and controlled, underneath we are a strange angry confused people. I think that is why we have so many secret societies.'

'Sadie, where is all this leading?' McIntyre asked, impatient as ever.

She wasn't offended. She gave him her sweet smile and answered, 'Because I think one of our secret societies is behind all this business. In Japan there are liberal secret societies, anti-liberal ones, left-wing secret societies and right-wing ones. But the most powerful secret societies are those involving the military. One of those alone has assassinated two of our prime ministers who didn't agree with their policies since the war, plus a foreign minister and the minister attached to the Imperial Court. Our present Prime Minister General Tanaka is a member of that society. Recently he said something like this: for settling difficulties in East Asia, Japan must adopt a policy of Blood and Iron ... in order to conquer the world, Japan must conquer Europe and Asia. In order to conquer Europe and Asia, Japan must first conquer China.'

'I say,' Dickie Bird exclaimed, 'bit different from the masons, your secret societies, Sadie.'

'Very,' she said, face suddenly hard and set. 'Now with a blood-thirsty Prime Minister like that the military secret societies feel they have the go-ahead, whatever international public opinion might think to the contrary, to trick Japan into a war with China. I was going to be the incident. As a distant relative of the emperor, there would be no other course open to our country but to fight China. The way would be open to the conquest of the world.'

'So Captain Moto, who got all this thing rolling, is a member of that military secret society,' McIntyre snapped.

'Exactly,' Sadie answered and added, 'my would-be fiancé, the General, too. Moto wouldn't have acted without orders from him.'

Smith whistled softly. 'It sounds very rich, Sadie, but it rings true. Your family ordered you to marry him. He invited you to Shanghai, where the redbeards of Mr Chen here,' he indicated the Chinese with his impassive face and dark eyes which revealed nothing, 'kidnapped you at Captain Moto's command.'

'Very rich,' she agreed. 'So rich that it makes me sick to my stomach! I had been lured into a kidnap and murder plot for the sake of Greater Nippon. How cynical they all are.' She gave a bitter laugh.

Dickie Bird felt his heart go out to her at this moment. 'Don't take on, Sadie,' he said encouragingly.

'But I do, Dickie. Now I am an embarrassment to them all, right up to the very top, including General Tanaka.'

'How do you mean?' Smith asked quickly.

'This. Neither in Shanghai or back in Osaka in Japan, where my family live, will I be safe any more. I know too much.'

'You mean they'll kill you?'

'Yes.'

Dickie Bird looked very worried. 'What will you do?' he asked.

But before Sadie could answer that question, the lookout at the bow sang, 'Small town coming up, sir. Looks all right to me, sir.'

Smith stood up and focused his glasses. With them he swept the place, a square of one-storey buildings for the most part. As far as he could see there were no soldiers on the little stone jetty. 'We need water,' he said, for they had been drinking Bass light ale for the last twenty-four hours; their water tank was empty. Even Billy Bennett who was a great beer drinker had complained. 'No ruddy char! Yer ordinary matelot can't live without his mug o'char.' Besides they needed water too for the boilers. They still had a hundred fifty miles of the Yangtze. 'Right, Dickie, you'll be in charge and see the men are armed. Major McIntyre and Mr Chen would you come with me and Ginger. We'll see about filling our tanks.'

'Yes,' McIntyre snapped. 'But we'll have to keep our weather eye open. In China you can trust no one, it seems.'

Mr Chen behind him gave a little weary smile, but said nothing. McIntyre was almost right, but one day it would be different, he knew.

A quarter of an hour later they were nosing their way at a snail's pace through muddy water, filth-laden with human faeces and rotting vegetation – and the body of a child, probably that of a girl, thrown into the river as an unwanted mouth. On the jetty, barefoot porters in the godowns stopped their work to watch them. But their broad yellow faces showed nothing but idle curiosity.

They tied up and CPO Ferguson looked threateningly at the ragged beggars coming towards them already, begging bowls at the ready. 'Bugger off, ye heathen devils,' he snorted, 'and dinna dare touch my boat.'

The beggars obviously didn't understand a word of English, but the old Scot's tone sufficed. They limped away, muttering surlily among themselves. 'All right, Dickie,' Smith said with a smile, 'we're off. You're in charge.'

'Good show,' Dickie chortled. 'Don't talk to any strange ladies, Smithie.'

'See if you can get any taties, sir,' Billy Bennett pleaded, 'I'm sick to death of that rice stuff.'

'I'll try. Come on, Major and Mr Chen.' The three of them sprang onto the jetty and the Chinese porters backed off to let them through, some of them touching their horny hands to the foreheads as a sign of respect.

Mr Chen gave the porters a stiff little bow, shot a question at them in Chinese and, turning to the two white men, translated the answer he had received. 'They say there is a kind of ship's chandler at the end of jetty, gentlemen. He will supply us with what we need.'

'Good,' Smith said, and touched the money belt filled with gold sovereigns beneath his shirt. 'I think the Horsemen of St George will suffice.'

'Horsemen of St George?' McIntyre queried him, as they walked, pushing their way through the beggars and loungers, their nostrils again full of that stench that seemed to be ever present in Chinese towns and cities.

'English gold sovereigns,' Smith answered.

The ship's chandler sat at the back of his dark store, writing on a piece of coarse paper with a black ink brush. He was fat and wore a black cotton robe. His cap was black, as well as his shoes, and he could have been taken for an undertaker, Smith told himself. Mr Chen said something and the man looked up to reveal a fat oily face and cunning dark eyes. He put down his brush immediately, rose and bowed and said something in Chinese. Mr Chen translated. 'The honourable merchant says that you will do him sublime favour if you take tea with him.' While Mr Chen spoke, the merchant rubbed his pudgy hands together all the time, as if he was washing them with a piece of invisible soap, smiling with a full set of gold teeth.

'We haven't got much time.' McIntyre began–

But Smith cut him short with, 'Yes, we'd better. That's the way they conduct business in China.'

The merchant clapped his hands and almost immediately, a youth appeared, who was a younger model of the merchant, bearing a teapot and handleless cups on a bamboo tray. The merchant said something, the boy bowed, poured the tea without a word and disappeared. But as he went through the beaded curtain into the store, McIntyre caught a fleeting glimpse of the look on his face. It was one of evil intent. Automatically his hand slipped down to the pocket of his tunic and felt the heavy metal lump of his Colt. Something fishy might be going on, he told himself.

So they sipped the scalding hot green tea and discussed their needs, discovering that the ship's chandler's store contained that great rarity in China, some sacks of potatoes. 'He says,' Mr Chen translated with a faint smile on his face, 'that he keeps them for the foreign gentlemen who pass this way – actually he said foreign barbarians who know nothing of good Chinese rice.' Mr Chen shrugged slightly. 'No matter. He will sell them to us – for gold.'

'He looks as if he'd sell his goddam mother for gold,' McIntyre commented sourly, his mind on the look on the youth's unsavoury face.

Five minutes later the tea was finished and they commenced haggling in the Chinese fashion about prices. McIntyre excused himself, leaving Mr Chen and Smith to it, while he went outside into the warm sunny afternoon. He looked around suspiciously. The youth had disappeared. But McIntyre supposed he could have gone off for the merchant on some kind of errand. But still he was nagged by doubt.

He took out a crumpled pack of cigarettes, lit one and started to stroll aimlessly down the jetty. The coolies made way for him and the beggars made no attempt to ask for alms. They knew instinctively that the white man with the craggy battered face was not a man to be trifled with.

McIntyre came to the edge of the jetty. He puffed moodily at his cheap cigarette and stared out over the great river. A flight of cranes was streaming low over the river heading west. There was the usual collection of junks and sampans. Then he noticed the motorboat, a very decrepit old craft trailing soot and black smoke behind it. It struck him suddenly as strange. Who would have a motorboat in this one-horse town, he asked himself. 'Hell,' he said aloud, talking to himself in the manner of lonely, withdrawn men, 'where would they get the gas for its engine in this arsehole of the world?'

Suddenly McIntyre threw his burning cigarette into the dirty brown water of the Yangtze. With the instant recognition of a vision, he knew who was in that ancient motorboat. The kid with the evil face. He was going somewhere to tell, whoever he was to meet, that they were in the little one-horse town. McIntyre didn't know who that was, and he didn't care. What he did know, however, was that the kid spelled trouble.

Hurriedly he strode back to the chandler's store where Smith and the others were just emerging from the door. He told Smith his suspicions and then snapped in a low voice, while the merchant beamed at him, showing those gold teeth of his, 'Come on, Smith, let's make it snappy. Get those stores and water aboard toot sweet.'

In the last week or so Smith had seen enough of what went on in China to know the big Canadian might well be right. He turned to the smiling merchant and said in what he took to be the Chinese phrase for hurry, 'Chop chop!'

The merchant bowed and clapped his hands. Immediately the barefoot dockers started to run in a kind of shuffling trot back and forth between the pinnace and the merchant's godown carrying the water and potatoes, plus a few odds and ends which Smith had ordered, while McIntyre stared downstream wondering what kind of trouble they were in for now. Next to him, Ginger tensed, rifle at the ready.

Chapter Nine

'Well,' Captain Moto demanded, as the ancient motorboat chugged away, trailing smoke behind it, 'are you prepared to help me, Commander?'

The little captain looked at the Intelligence Officer coldly. 'I have already informed you, Captain Moto, I take my orders from the Commander-in-Chief of the Imperial Japanese Navy.' He sucked in his breath sharply in deference to that august person in far-off Tokyo.

'But you have heard what the boy had to say,' Moto protested. 'The interpreter said he told him he had seen the foreign devils and Princess Sadako. Now is the time to act before she reaches Shanghai and reveals all she undoubtedly knows. Then everything will fall apart.'

Lt. Commander Hashimoto was unimpressed. 'That is your problem. I am in command of this ship and I see it my duty to obey orders that are legitimate and come from my *legitimate* superiors.' He gave the angry Intelligence man a look of contempt. 'I will not be party to some hare-brained scheme hatched by a lot of hot-heads in Tokyo.'

Moto swallowed hard as if trying to control his savage temper. 'But don't you see, Commander? This is for the sake of our beloved Nippon. If we can force a war between ourselves and those rotten Chinese, it will be the first step on our path to the conquest of the world. Hasn't our Prime Minister himself, General Tanaka, said so? There is no time to be lost. We must act now.'

The little captain remained unmoved by Moto's words. He said, 'I am afraid you must be deaf, Captain Moto. If I am ordered to war by my superiors, I shall go joyfully. If I am to die, I shall do that also joyfully for the sake of our beloved Nippon.' He drew his breath in reverently. 'But I certainly will take no part in the murder of a woman who is related to his Imperial Majesty.' He turned in the direction of where he thought Tokyo was and bowed low.

Captain Moto's dark eyes blazed beneath his thick, horn-rimmed spectacles. 'Then you shall die,' he said to himself. 'He who is not with us is against us and must pay the penalty.'

Without another word, Moto saluted and turned stiffly to march away to the far end of the awning where a group of younger officers had been watching the exchange. They clicked to attention as Moto approached. Swiftly he ordered them to stand at ease, and then said, 'He will not do it. He is sticking strictly to the rules.'

There were angry murmurs from the young officers, who knew now what was going on. One of them hissed, 'He must be made to do what you require, Captain Moto. Japan's future is at stake.'

'Exactly,' another said.

Captain Moto held up his pudgy, sweating hands for silence. 'What is the attitude of the crew?' he asked.

Someone laughed as if it were an absurd question. 'In the Japanese Imperial Navy,' he said, 'the crew do as they are told. Or else.'

Some of the others laughed too.

'The next senior officer?' Moto asked.

The smiles vanished from the young men's faces. 'He is the same as Commander Hashimoto,' one of them ventured. 'He will stick to the rules. He would regard anything done against the Captain's authority as mutiny, Captain Moto.'

Captain Moto gave them his dangerous smile, the eyes cold and threatening behind the thick spectacles. 'Then, gentlemen, I think we must instigate a mutiny. Are you with me?'

As one, the young officers, their faces gleaming with excitement, clicked to attention and rasped, *'Hi!'*

'Good,' Moto snapped, very businesslike now, 'fetch your weapons. I shall deal with Commander Hashimoto personally.' He touched the hilt of his samurai sword significantly, as the officers saluted and hurried away.

While he waited for them to return, he eyed the bridge where Commander Hashimoto was talking with his second-in-command standing behind the helmsman. The gunboat was proceeding at a snail's pace for, as always, Commander Hashimoto, a prudent man, was attempting to save fuel by sailing at this speed. It would look good on his record when they got to Shanghai. Moto approved. It meant the English boat wouldn't be too far behind. This day he wanted the business over with. General Tanaka and the rest were chomping at the bit. They wanted the war started. Already the key assault infantry divisions were in their barracks in Tokyo, fully armed and ready to march. The troop transports which would take the infantry to China were already at anchor at Nigata. On their airfields the bomber and fighter pilots, all eager to carry out their planned missions, were on red alert. Now the only thing which stood in all their ways was this damned obscure little naval officer. He felt that familiar red rage begin to burn within him. The hand gripping the butt of his sword was wet with sweat and his heart had commenced pounding madly.

One after another the young officers appeared, faces flushed, eyes gleaming with excitement. All of them had pistol belts buckled around their waists. One of them had abandoned his white naval cap and had tied the red and white sash of a samurai around his cropped head. Captain Moto nodded his approval. 'Good, then we march,' he snapped. 'Come on.'

He turned and began to march to the bridge, trailing the absurdly long sword behind him. They followed, breath coming in hectic excited gasps. Noisily they clattered up the companion-way to the bridge. Moto opened the door and Hashimoto swung round. He saw them standing there. Probably he guessed what was happening, but his face showed no fear. Indeed his look was one of anger. 'What's this?' he demanded. 'Why are you on my bridge when you're not on duty?' Behind him his second-in-command looked afraid, but he nodded his head firmly, as if in agreement with the captain.

'I shall ask you formally,' Moto said, restraining his burning hot temper with difficulty, 'are you with us? Or not?'

'And I shall tell you equally formally,' Commander Hashimoto answered, 'I am not taking orders from you.'

Moto's eyes blazed. 'You officers will report to me at fifteen hundred hours,' Hashimoto continued, appearing to have forgotten the little army officer. 'I shall have a few words to say to you about your conduct at this moment. And you, Ensign, take off that ribbon. Fetch your official cap *immediately!*' There was iron in the Commander's voice now.

Meekly the young ensign began to untie the band around his cropped head.

Moto sensed the resolve of the young officers was weakening. He had to act – at once. 'You refuse!' he cried in a choked voice. 'Then pay the penalty.' He drew his great curved sword. The Captain's face blanched. He staggered back a few paces, hands extended in front of him as if ready to ward off any blow.

Moto gave a deep grunt which seemed to come from his belly. He thrust out one foot and whirled the sword around his head. It gleamed momentarily in the sun. Next moment he slashed it across the Captain's neck. The Captain gave one shrill scream of absolute pain. Next moment his headless body crumpled to the spotless deck, while the bloody head trundled to the side of the bridge and lay there like some child's abandoned football.

Moto, his chest heaving with the effort, advanced another pace to the horrified second-in-command, the blood gleaming and dripping from the blade of his sword.

'And you,' he grunted thickly, 'what will you do, Lieutenant?'

The second-in-command flashed a look to the headless body of his captain lying crumpled on the deck of the bridge, his lifeblood beginning to stain the scrubbed planks of that deck. 'I ... I don't know...' he began to stutter.

'Shut your mouth!' Moto ordered him harshly, both hands still firmly gripping the hilt of the sword, his knuckles white with the effort. 'If you want to live join us. Well?'

Slowly the second-in-command nodded. He was too afraid to speak.

Moto lowered his sword, feeling his shirt sticking to him unpleasantly, wet with sweat as it was. 'You're the temporary captain,' he said a little contemptuously. 'Get rid of that traitor first.' He swung round, ignoring the new captain, and said, 'This is what we are going to do.' Swiftly he explained his plan of action, while two ratings came up on the bridge to bear the dead captain away, while another placed his bloody severed head in a pail and did the same.

The young officers listened intently until he was finished. Then one of them said, 'But Captain Moto if we kill them all including the Princess, how are we to convince the

Japanese people that the – er – dreadful deed has been done by the Chinks? What evidence of that will we have?'

Captain Moto smiled cruelly. 'I am glad you have asked that question, my young friend.'

At the rail the sailor was emptying the white enamel pail of Commander Hashimoto's severed head. It hit the water with a little splash, sank and then bobbed up again, face upwards so that it appeared the Captain was looking at them. The Ensign who had bound the samurai cloth around his forehead gave a little shudder and looked away swiftly.

Moto's cruel smile broadened. He told himself they would all see worse things than that before they were finished in the war which was soon to come. 'Now in answer to your question, my young friend. Of course the Princess must live – *for a while*. During that time we shall produce the evidence that the Japanese people needs to make them want to demand a war.' He let his words sink in and added a moment later, 'We shall dice for her.'

The young officers looked puzzled.

'We shall dice for her body,' he explained.

'For her body?' someone asked.

'Yes,' Moto answered calmly. 'For the pleasure of raping her.' They gasped.

'I am sure you are not averse to raping a member of the Imperial Royal Family,' Moto said and gave a reverent sigh. 'I can say that I wouldn't be, if I won the draw. In that way we are all implicated – *if anything goes wrong*.' He paused and added, voice so soft that they had to strain to catch his words, 'Naturally the one who has the pleasure of raping her must kill her.' He smiled evilly. 'I think that is quite clear, don't you?'

A heavy silence fell on the little group of officers. Moto repeated his statement. There came a reluctant chorus of 'yes'. Down in the water the Captain's head began to drift away. Yet the eyes in that upturned yellow face still seemed to be levelled at the young men, as if in silent reproach.

PART THREE

Nip And Tuck

Chapter One

'"*Comrade Stalin expects the most urgent action in this Chinese matter,*"' the full colonel of the NKVD, who had come all the way from Moscow to Leningrad to read the dictator's message to him, rasped out the words. '"*It is imperative that the Nationalists and Japanese Imperialists are involved in a war soon.*"' The full colonel looked up from the paper he was reading from and looked threateningly at Aronson. 'There is one more sentence on Comrade Chairman Stalin's message.'

Aronson, tall, blond and muscular, forced the look of obvious contempt from his handsome, clever face. It didn't do for a chief-of-intelligence to reveal his feelings to anyone, even a wife or a mistress – and he had both. That was how he had survived the Tsar's regime, that of the liberal idiot Kerensky, who had succeeded him, as well as Lenin's. Now he would survive the tyranny of Stalin, too. 'Then pray read it, Comrade Colonel,' he said politely, eyes wrinkled against the smoke of his cigarette.

'"*Failure to ensure this course of action will result in severe disciplinary action,*"' the NKVD colonel snapped, and added, 'Is that quite clear, Comrade?' Standing there in the middle of the office, tall and erect, with the green-topped cap of the Secret Police on his shaven head, he looked down severely at the man behind the desk.

Inwardly Aronson was laughing at the man. He was so pompous, so self-important. He probably thought that everyone pissed his pants when they were spoken to by a NKVD officer. Not him, though, not Aronson. Still he forced his face into a look of worried fear. '*Da, da, tvarovisch,*' he said hurriedly, '*Ponemayu...* I understand.'

The NKVD Colonel nodded as if he were satisfied with the impact he had made on this provincial chief-of-intelligence. He strode imperiously over to Aronson's littered desk and, taking hold of the table lighter without asking permission, snapped on the flame and burned the message over the ashtray. Finally he then crushed the ash. 'That message to you, Comrade, has never existed,' he said severely. 'Off the record I can tell you this. We, too, have interests in China. Our troops of the glorious Red Army are standing by to march into Manchuria, once the Imperialists and their lackeys go to war. It will be an easy victory for us.'

Aronson's heart missed a beat. That was the very last thing that Russia needed at this moment – another war. The country was in the midst of a terrible famine. There were dangers on all sides. Another war might well trigger off the third revolution in ten years.

The NKVD did not notice the look of alarm on the other man's face. 'I shall return to Moscow now by the midnight train. We expect an action report from you within the next forty-eight hours, Comrade.' He raised his clenched fist. Aronson sprang to his feet and did the same.

'All power to the people!' the NKVD Colonel barked the standard Party phrase of that year.

'All power to the people!' Aronson echoed it without enthusiasm.

A moment later the Colonel was gone, leaving Aronson with his thoughts, and they weren't pleasant. He slumped back in his chair and lit yet another cigarette. The HQ was quiet now. Only a few staff worked at night these days; they hadn't the physical strength. Outside it was snowing again and the streets were silent. Nobody but armed policemen ventured out onto the streets of Leningrad after dark. It was rumoured that there were abductors about once more who seized and killed easy victims and sold their flesh to the starving populace.

As he thought about these things, Aronson stared at his own image in the steel shaving mirror he kept on his desk. It was one of his few vanities, like his other mistress, a sixteen-year-old near-virgin who believed he was a counter-revolutionary dedicated to overthrowing Stalin. He didn't attempt to dissuade her. For he liked to play roles; he liked to play many roles just as he had many names, for Aronson wasn't his real one.

He stared harder at himself in the mirror. Aronson was a handsome man, but he didn't look at the mirror in order to reassure himself that he was. In fact, he stared at his reflection often to reassure himself that his true character never showed. Ever since he had been a boy he had made it a basic principle of his life that he must always conceal his true intentions and feelings from others. If he and those like him were ever going to save their beloved motherland from those fools, madmen and traitors who ruled her, it would have to be done by steely cunning. For Russia and its ordinary people, drunken, downtrodden lazy wretches that most of them were, had to survive. And it would be people like him who placed their country first and their private interests second who would ensure that Mother Russia *did* survive.

He took his eyes off his image in the mirror. Outside the silence was broken by the rumble of heavy wheels and the noise of the great iron doors to the rear of the HQ being opened. The trucks braked. There were hoarse shouts of *'davoi ... davoi ... move, you swine!'* Whips were cracked. Anderson told himself they were bringing more wretches for cross-examination. This was the time they brought them in, always after darkness had fallen so that the ordinary citizens of Leningrad could not see just how many 'reactionaries' and 'enemies of the state' there actually were.

A soft tap came at his door. He sat up. 'Come in,' he called.

It was Ilona, his spy in the HQ's radio room. Ilona, white blonde with a splendid, exciting figure and deep green eyes, thought, too, that he was some kind of reactionary, as she was, working undercover against the Soviet regime. She stood to attention at the door of the office, in case anyone was watching in the corridor and said, 'Message, Comrade Commissar.'

'Enter, Comrade,' he said sternly, as if this was an official matter.

She came in, giggled, wriggled her bottom provocatively and with her hands behind her back, locked the office door.

He smiled gently and asked, 'What is it?'

'We've just intercepted a message from that Yid – Borodin. He reports that those pigs, the Chink Communists, have dispatched a murder squad to liquidate that Japanese princess you told me about.' For the moment that look of sensual anticipation vanished from her beautiful face. 'Poor dear. Murdered for political reasons. It is a shame. You shouldn't let it happen, Dimitri.'

He rubbed his jaw and wished he had shaved. She had a very sensitive skin. 'Perhaps,' he said, as if talking to himself, 'I will try to stop it.'

'How?' she asked eagerly. 'I don't know what you can do from here.'

'I agree. But something will come to me.'

She gave a little sigh of relief and then her face brightened. 'I know what will come to you, darling – *me!*' Hurriedly she slipped out of her drab official skirt to reveal shapely silken thighs and black knickers trimmed with red lace.

He whistled softly with delight and said, 'Don't you know the new Soviet woman only wears cotton next to her pure skin? Silk is for decadent plutocrats, and reactionaries.'

She laughed easily. 'Then I'm a reactionary. Now will you come and help me to get out of this decadent, plutocratic underwear?'

She had taken his tongue in her mouth, sucking at it savagely, as if ravenous with hunger. He had felt himself harden immediately. At once he had broken out in a sweat. She had parted his legs and had begun jerking him. He had panted like a wild dog. He had wanted to penetrate her, thrust himself with savage fury into her body, but she had kept him waiting, tugging at him all the time. He could feel her breasts slapping his muscular chest, wet with sweat. Suddenly he had not been able to contain himself any longer. He had pushed away her hand, thrust her beneath him and parted her legs. With a savage grunt he had thrust himself into that delightful, burning moist hole.

So they had writhed and bucked, grunting

the foulest of obscenities, thrusting at each other as if they wanted to hurt the other person, bodies lathered in hot sweat, gasping for breath, the world outside forgotten for a while, concerned solely with their own animal pleasures.

Now they lay in each other's arms, smoking and staring at the peeling ceiling, listening to the soft hush of the new snow falling outside – content, happy, wordless. For a while.

The squeak of brakes, the hoarse cries, muted a little by the snow, the crack of whips, the yelps of pain, which heralded the arrival of a fresh group of political prisoners woke them to the grim reality of life in Soviet Russia. Aronson stubbed out his cigarette almost angrily, as she nuzzled closer to his chest, her eyes pressed tightly closed, now, as if she wished to blot out the world outside.

But he could not. Mother Russia was in danger once more. He had to think of some way to stop what was soon to happen in China. But what? That country was so far away. Borodin, the pederast, had set the wheels in motion, which would lead to the assassination of the Japanese Princess. How could he, here in Leningrad, stop it and prevent Russia being embroiled in yet another war, which might ruin her completely?

He pondered the problem, as down below the noise died away with the wretched prisoners being led away to the cells and torture chambers. Her hand had fallen to his loins. But he pretended not to notice it – he had to keep his mind clear.

Could Borodin do anything, he wondered, as her cunning little fingers toyed playfully with his flaccid member. He doubted if his agent could stop the murder squads, once they had been alerted for action, which they had, or so Borodin had reported. Then he had it, or he thought he had. He started to think his plan out, as he felt his loins begin to thicken under her devilish little hands.

Borodin wouldn't like it, of course. Naturally he would protest he was working against the interests and intention of Comrade Stalin. But Aronson told himself Borodin would *have* to like it and carry out his orders. He could blackmail the agent in Nanking relentlessly if he wished and Borodin knew that. He'd do as he was told.

Now she was tracing a way down his body with her wet lips, kissing and licking his nipples, screwing her wet tongue into his belly button. He shivered a little with delight and anticipation. He knew what she was going to do.

It was the only way to save the Japanese woman. Naturally he knew that it would cost him his head if it ever came out – Stalin was absolutely ruthless – but he had to take the risk for the sake of Russia. The English must be warned. Then he forgot them and the unknown Japanese aristocrat, as he looked down at her. How beautiful her white hand looked as she held him there, as if she were holding a flower. Her mouth descended upon him.

Chapter Two

Billy Bennett opened his mouth and belched happily. 'Blimey, Ginger,' he said, as they nosed their way down the great river, 'that did hit the spot. Taties and bully beef hash! You can't beat grub like that, old mate.'

Ginger sniffed and looked at the darkening water. 'All right then, you've filled yer guts. Don't rabbit on about it. Man don't live for food alone, yer knows.' He grabbed the front of his trousers to make his point quite clear. 'Yer ordinary matelot needs a bit of the other every now and agen.'

Billy Bennett laughed easily. ''Fraid yer'll have to wait till Shanghai for a bit o' that – open them pearly gates.' He sucked a fragment of potato out of his front teeth and added, 'Hope there's taties and bangers for breakfast.'

Ginger Kerrigan shook his head and gave up on his shipmate.

Up on the forrard deck, watching the little villages and hamlets on the port-side vanishing slowly into the evening darkness, Dickie Bird, unusually serious for him, asked the Princess, 'What do you think you'll do once we get to Shanghai, Sadie?'

Sadie looked at the handsome young sailor, as if she were seeing him for the very first time. Now she saw that the Englishman could not conceal his adoration for her and she was flattered. At college she had dated young Americans, but they had all been too immature for her and at the back of her mind there had always been her father's warning: 'Remember, my dear, you must marry the man your father picks for you. That is your duty, always think of that.' So there had been just harmless flirtations, which had culminated in her father's order to marry the general, who was twice her age, perhaps even older. She sighed. 'I don't really know, Dickie,' she said slowly. 'Because of what I now know I am being forced into a kind of exile. There is no going back.'

'But where will you go, Sadie?' Dickie persisted. 'And how will you support yourself, if I may ask?'

'The second question is easy to answer. I have money of my own. The first is very difficult to answer.' She frowned.

'Would you consider England?' Dickie ventured, feeling himself going red even as he asked the question.

'I don't–' she began, but didn't complete her answer.

In that moment the lookout at the bow sang out, 'Craft to starboard, sir! ... Two hundred yards away.'

On the bridge next to CPO Ferguson, Smith swung up his glasses. He focused them hurriedly. The light was bad. He wanted the greatest possible magnification.

'What do you make of her, sir?' CPO Ferguson asked urgently.

For a moment Smith didn't answer, then he moaned, 'That's torn it! It's the Jap gunboat ... and the forrard gun crew is closed up, looking ready for action.'

CPO Ferguson whistled. 'D'ye mean, sir, yon craft's gonna take a crack at us?'

'It certainly looks like it.' Automatically he pressed the alarm button. The klaxon shrieked and the off-duty watch started to tumble out, pulling on their sea clothes as they did so. 'Man the guns!' Smith yelled above the racket as on the Japanese ship a searchlight clicked on abruptly. Its beam started to sweep the darkening water. It was followed an instant later by a star shell which exploded with a sharp crack above the pinnace, bathing her in glowing icy white light.

Down below Dickie Bird hurried a suddenly pale-faced Sadie into the wardroom, crying above the noise, 'You'll be all right, Sadie. Don't worry.' A moment later he was pushing his way through the off-duty watch to the bridge, where McIntyre and Mr Chen had already taken up their positions.

Now all of them stared in awed fascination at the advancing Japanese gunboat, as it bore down upon them slowly, almost majestically, the white-clad gunners in position behind their weapon.

'The Nips mean business,' McIntyre

concluded. 'Moto must have got them steamed up to break international law and have a crack at us.'

'What does international law mean to them?' Dickie Bird asked bitterly. 'We're going to disappear anyway. No one will be one jot the wiser.'

'Shut up, Dickie please,' Smith said. 'We've got to do something – and quick.' He thrust up his glasses again and peered at the opposite bank, perhaps half a mile away. 'I can't hear myself bloody think.'

McIntyre raised his glasses, too. Swiftly he swept the darkening shore. 'There's an inlet,' he began.

The night stillness was ripped apart by the shriek of a shell. It zipped over the pinnace and exploded some fifty feet to the port side, throwing up a huge gout of water. For a moment their craft rocked back and forth dangerously.

'Christ,' Dickie Bird cried, 'they're ranging in. They really are going to have a crack at us.'

Smith's mind raced. They, too, had a cannon, but he doubted if it would be much use against the thickly-armoured hull of the Japanese gunboat. 'Ginger,' he cried, as the enemy gun cracked into violent life once more, 'sweep their forrard deck with bullets.'

'Ay ay, sir,' Ginger Kerrigan yelled back cheerfully and pressed his trigger.

Again the Japanese gunboat fired. The shell zapped low across the river. Next instant it exploded only some twenty feet away from the pinnace. The craft keeled over violently. For a moment the bridge seemed to touch the surface of the river. Then it righted itself, instruments and the like slithering back and forth.

'Christ Almighty,' McIntyre cursed. 'That was bloody close!'

On the 'monkey island' behind the bridge, Ginger pressed his trigger. Tracer zipped lethally towards the gunboat. The observers could see the angry blue sparks flying as the slugs hit the armour-plated sides of the gunboat. Ginger raised his sights and swept the craft's deck. A crewman flung up his arms dramatically. Next moment he pitched forward over the side and into the water. He didn't come up. But a frustrated Ginger was unable to get at the guncrew. They were protected by the weapon's armoured shield and his slugs howled off it harmlessly like glowing golf balls. 'Frig it all,' he cursed through clenched teeth, 'swing the frigging thing round so I can frigging well get at yer!'

But the Japanese gun crew stubbornly refused to oblige him so the machine-gunner turned his attention on the low bridge, peppering the superstructure with a vicious hail of fire.

Below him Smith made his decision. 'They've almost cooked our goose,' he yelled above the racket. 'I'm going to make a run for that inlet over there. I'm hoping that the draught is too shallow for the Japs to follow us in.

'But Smithie,' Dickie objected, 'once we're in there, they've got–' he ducked hurriedly as another shell hissed frighteningly above the pinnace and exploded only yards away showering the small craft with tons of water, '–us trapped. We're up the creek without a paddle. All they have to do is to wait for us to come out.'

'I'll worry about that when the time comes. But let's get the hell out of here – *fast!*' He spoke into the voice tube. The engine-room responded immediately. The pinnace's sharp prow rose out of the water. Under his feet Smith could feel the deck vibrating, as the engines shrieked and rose to full power. Behind them they threw up a sudden wild white wake. The pinnace surged forward, the Japanese shells falling behind her. She was escaping for the time being.

Behind them, standing on the bridge of the gunboat next to the new captain, Captain Moto lowered his glasses and smiled evilly. 'Now,' he announced to no one in particular, 'they are ours for the taking.'

'But Captain Moto,' the naval officer said, 'I don't think we have the draught to follow them up that inlet.'

Moto shrugged carelessly. 'We shall try, won't we?' There was iron in his voice suddenly and he tightened his grip on that absurd samurai sword of his.

The other officer saw the gesture and remembered what had happened to Commander Hashimoto. 'Yes, yes, of course,' he said hurriedly. He bent and spoke into the voice tube. Below, the engine-room responded. The gunboat's speed picked up. The craft started to follow the fleeing British pinnace, the gunners still firing though their target was rapidly diminishing.

Now the gunboat was very close to the shore. Here and there in the far distance, Moto could see the twinkle of lights but around the inlet there was no sign of human habitation. He told himself that was all to the good. The Chinese were less than filth – of no account whatsoever. All the same it was better that there were no witnesses of what was going to happen this night.

He let his mind dwell on what was to come, feeling a sudden sexual desire. There was a 'good time' girl on board who pleasured the crew. But he didn't fancy that raddled whore who serviced a dozen men a day. He thought of the Princess. She would undoubtedly be a virgin. In Japan all girls of high rank entered marriage as virgins. He licked his thick lips, eyes glistening behind the thick glasses, as he visualized ripping the clothes off her, forcing her legs apart and then thrusting into her, as she screamed and struggled and tried to fight him off. Perhaps he might be lucky in the draw soon to come.

'Lieutenant,' he said thickly, trying to repress the sudden lust that ran through his body like fire, 'I am going to the wardroom to speak to your officers. You're in charge.'

'Yes, Captain Moto,' the new skipper said dutifully, eyeing the dark shore anxiously. The draught was getting shallower by the metre. 'I understand.'

Captain Moto was in a high good mood, as he faced the young officers in the wardroom. He raised his cup of *saki* and said, 'Let me give you a toast. "To the coming war. *Banzai!*" He drained the rice wine in one gulp.

They responded as one. *'Banzai,'* they roared in their hoarse enthusiastic young voices. They drained their cups, too.

Moto beamed at them through his thick glasses. He said, 'Gentlemen the time has come for us to decide who is going to do the – er – dirty deed. To the Princess, I mean.' He beamed even more.

The young officers, flushed and excited as they were at the thought of the coming war, looked sombre now. The prospect of raping a member of the Royal Family went against their sense of honour. After all, anyone who was related to his Imperial Majesty, a god in his own right, would be divine herself.

Moto's smile vanished. 'It has to be done,' he snapped firmly. 'Realize that. More is at stake than the fate of a foolish Americanized woman. Here are the dice. The lowest —' His words were drowned by the sound of grinding, rending metal. Abruptly the gunboat came to a stop and listed slightly to one side.

'Damn,' one of the officers yelled, leaping to his feet, *'we've run aground.'*

Chapter Three

They had heard the crash, followed by the furious racing of the Japanese gunboat's engines, followed by a loud echoing silence, and had guessed what had happened. 'Jolly good show,' Dickie Bird had chortled happily. 'The Nips have gorn and run aground. Topping, what?'

McIntyre had reacted in that typically sour manner of his, with, 'Yeah, so they can't come in. But remember this, Bird, we can't get *out* either.'

Half an hour later they had sent Mr Chen down the inlet to do a reconnaissance. He had gone without a protest, though he knew the Japanese would shoot him out of hand – what was a Chinese's life worth! – if they discovered him.

Now he was back and they crowded around him in the tiny wardroom to listen to what he had to relate. It wasn't too much, but even as he explained the situation of the gunboat, Smith was beginning to dream up a bold idea.

'The Japanese gentlemen are firmly stuck on the right bank at the entrance to the inlet,' Mr Chen was saying in that excellent English sing-song voice of his. 'Now all is tranquil on board their ship.'

'So they are not attempting to refloat her?' Smith interjected quickly.

'It does not appear to be the case,' Mr Chen replied in his usual oblique manner. 'All is silent. Naturally the river will do it for them in the morning, undoubtedly,' he added blandly.

'What do you mean, Mr Chen?' McIntyre asked.

'It is the manner of the river, Major McIntyre. The Yangtze has tides, or sudden increases in the depth of the water, sometimes as much as forty feet.'

Dickie Bird whistled softly and Smith said, 'I've noticed, especially where there are narrows.'

'Yes,' Mr Chen went on, 'ignorant no-good Chinese peasants call them river spirits. They are afraid of them because they cannot explain the sudden changes in the water level. So the Japanese gentlemen can expect the river to float them off sometime tomorrow morning.' He gave a little shrug and said, 'Unfortunately our Chinese river will help the enemy this time. It is sad.'

At any other time Smith would have laughed at the plump little yellow man's quaint statement, but not now. His mind was racing electrically with his daring scheme.

'So that means,' McIntyre was saying, glancing at his watch and noting it was nearly midnight, 'we've got about ten hours or so to get out of this mess.' He turned to the two naval officers. 'Does this inlet lead back into the river somewhere or other?' he asked.

Dickie Bird looked at Smith and when the latter didn't answer, said, 'No, I've been over the charts with a fine-tooth comb. This particular inlet peters out in about five miles from here and there are no side-arms leading anywhere in particular off it. No,' he concluded and bit his bottom lip as he looked across at the Princess, 'I'm afraid this is a dead end.'

'Yeah,' McIntyre said harshly, 'dead end is the right word for it and we're gonna be the dead ones, if we can–'

'Listen,' Smith cut in softly.

They turned and stared at him. Outside all was silent save for the steady tread of the lookout on the deck above and the persistent croaking of the bullfrogs in the reeds on the bank. A damp fog was rising in the night cold and everything was muffled, muted.

'The Nips are waiting for the morrow, obviously knowing that they've got us by the short and curlies and that they can play a waiting game—' Suddenly Smith remembered Sadie was present and blushing he said, 'Please accept my apologies, Sadie.'

She smiled sweetly and said, 'I've heard worse.'

'Well,' Smith continued, 'I'm hoping that the Nips will be relaxing off their guard, sleeping and waiting for tomorrow before they take further action. Perhaps they are planning to send boarding parties up the inlet if we won't come out. Perhaps they will attempt to starve us out.'

'But Smithie,' Dickie Bird objected, 'they could think we'd abandon the pinnace and go it back to Shanghai on foot.'

Smith shook his head. 'I doubt it. They'd reason the distance is too far and through dangerous country. Besides they'd think the Princess here wouldn't be capable of it.'

Sadie laughed. 'I held the track record at college for middle distance running. I'm pretty fit.'

Smith smiled at her and said, 'I'm sure you are. But they don't know that.' His smile vanished. 'Now I think our only chance is to take the attack to them during the hours of darkness.'

'How do you mean?' McIntyre asked urgently. 'We're stuck up this bloody creek.'

'The pinnace might be stuck, Major, but we aren't. We're mobile.'

'But what can you attack the gunboat with,' McIntyre persisted, 'a peashooter? The only heavy armament we have is the six-pounder and it's firmly attached to the deck. Or do you think we could carry it, eh?' He laughed cynically.

'No,' Smith answered coolly, 'but we could carry some of the six-pounder's shells.'

'But what the Sam Hill good would that do – without the six-pounder?' McIntyre snorted impatiently.

Smith told him and the others. When he was finished, McIntyre whistled softly. Dickie Bird said. 'Oh my sainted aunt, what a cracking idea!'

Mr Chen added, 'Very dangerous in my humble opinion, but good, Mr Smith.'

Smith smiled at them. 'Now we haven't got any time to lose.' He turned to CPO Ferguson. 'Get on to Mac,' he meant the pinnace's engineer, 'and put him in the picture. He can show Billy Bennett, he's our biggest chap, how to fix the shells... Dickie, you'll be in charge of the rest of the crew.'

Bird pulled a face because he wasn't going with the boarding party, but said nothing.

'McIntyre and you, Mr Chen, I'd like you to come with us, if you would.'

McIntyre gave one of those tough grins of his and said, 'Try and stop us.'

'Good, now I'm off to pick the boarding party.' And with that he was gone out into the foggy night.

Now things moved fast. Mac and Billy Bennett laboured mightily, fixing the big six-inch shells, as Smith had ordered. Explosive charges were attached. Then it was the turn of the boat crew to muster, six ratings, including Ginger Kerrigan with a detached Lewis gun cradled in his arms, pans of ammunition, hanging by straps from his belt. Grunting and panting, Billy Bennett carried the shells to the waiting boat and lowered them very carefully into its belly. Finally he went down below to the locker and re-appeared moments later with a coil of fuse wire wrapped around his shoulder.

By one o'clock that morning they were all

ready. Smith did a final check that all the men were correctly armed and were carrying one of the old-fashioned cutlasses as well. Then he went over to where Sadie and Dickie Smith stood in the wet fog, touched his cap in salute, saying, 'Now look after the pinnace and Sadie.'

'In that order of importance I suppose,' she said with a soft chuckle.

Smith blushed and said, 'Sorry about that.'

Her beautiful face was suddenly serious. 'Look after yourself, all of you,' she breathed.

'Don't worry. Can't keep a good fellow down.' Smith turned and ordered, 'Lower away.'

Hastily the rowing boat was lowered over the side and entered the water with a slight splash. Carefully Smith lowered himself into the boat and said to CPO Ferguson, who was acting as helmsman, 'All right, Chiefie take her away.'

The ratings bent their backs and took the strain. The oars had been muffled with strips of blankets and they made hardly a sound, as the little craft began to pull away, watched by those on deck in silence.

Moments later they had disappeared into

the wet fog. A few seconds later the soft splash of six pairs of oars in the water had vanished, too.

At Dickie Bird's side, the Princess shivered slightly, whether from fear or cold, Dickie didn't know. Instinctively he pressed her soft hand. She returned the pressure. She said, 'Dickie, you're very kind and sweet to me. I don't know why. I've been such a bother to you and the rest of your fellows.' She paused, as if hesitating to say what she was going to say, then she said it, 'You know, those men around General Tanaka are crazy – *I* think they are at least – but they mean to carry out their plan to involve Imperial Japan in a war.' She looked at Dickie Bird directly. 'That will mean that one day my country will fight your country... How would you feel about that in regard to us?'

Dickie Bird knew what she meant. It indicated that she was thinking about him, about the two of them together. 'I don't know,' he stuttered, caught completely off guard. 'All I know is that if two people – er, like – each other they can overcome all difficulties, even the greatest.'

She smiled. 'Dickie, you say the nicest things. But let's postpone any more talk on this matter. Let's worry about the present first. But, if you like,' now she was hesitant, 'you can kiss me.'

'Can I?' Dickie Bird breathed.

Thus they clung to each other in the wet fog like two rather frightened children, wondering what will happen next.

Chapter Four

There was hardly a sound. Even the frogs seemed to have stopped croaking. Carefully, the six oarsmen rowed the little boat through the fog, with McIntyre and Smith at the bow staring anxiously to their front, trying to catch the first glimpse of the stranded Japanese gunboat.

Now it was almost two in the morning and Smith guessed the Japanese crew would be fast asleep in their bunks. Even the engine-room staff would be asleep, now that they couldn't use their engines. In essence then, the raiders would have to contend with the lookouts only.

It seemed that McIntyre could read Smith's thoughts, for he leaned closer to the latter and whispered into his ear, 'How many lookouts do you think the Nips will have?'

'Four is my guess,' Smith whispered back, 'at bow and stern and two at midships, to port and starboard. My main worry is the one at the stern.'

'Do you want me to nobble him before you start?' McIntyre hissed.

'Do you think you can manage it?'

'Sure,' the big Canadian answered easily, 'just like falling off a log. We did it all the time in the last show when we raided the Hun trenches. One guy nobbled the sentry, then we cut the wire and we were in. They will have dropped anchor, won't they?'

'Yes,' Smith whispered. 'They will have done to prevent her drifting further onto the bank.'

'Good. Then that's my way up. Up the anchor chain–' He stopped short. 'There she is, Smith – the Nip!'

Smith strained his eyes and peered through the drifting fog. Then he, too, saw the stranded ship's riding lights. They were dim, but they were there all right. 'Ship oars,' he hissed urgently.

As one, the crew drew their oars out of the water and reached for their weapons. Now the little boat started to drift with the current, heading straight for the gunboat, each man hardly daring to breathe. For all of them knew that their lives would be forfeit if they were spotted at this range.

Smith waited tensely, as they drew level with the silent ship. Each man had ducked now in order not to make too large a silhouette. All the same it took only for the bow lookout to glance over the side and see them, despite the fog.

He reached out and grabbed for the ship's hull. Next to him CPO Ferguson did the same. They halted the progress of the little rowing boat and with their hands, muscles bulging with the effort, brows dripping with sweat in spite of the night cold, they propelled themselves forward so close to the curved hull of the gunboat that the midships lookout wouldn't be able to spot them.

They reached the anchor chain, after what seemed an age, the two men gasping, as if they had just run a great race. With the help of the others, Smith held the little rowing boat at the chain. He nodded to McIntyre. The latter nodded back. He pulled his Colt from its holster and stuck it loose into his belt – just in case. Gingerly he caught hold of the anchor chain and put his right foot on one of the rungs. It clanked noisily and he froze where he was, heart beating like a trip hammer, waiting for the first cry of alarm. Nothing! McIntyre wet his suddenly dry lips. He took hold once more and stepped onto the next rung. It clanked, but not so noisily. Gingerly, very gingerly, he began to ascend the chain, feeling it swing and bend beneath his weight, praying that he wouldn't be spotted before he reached the deck. He wasn't.

Carefully, he took a hold of the stern rail and peered over it. The deck was shrouded in fog and for a few moments, as he studied it, he thought there wasn't a lookout there. Then he smelled tobacco smoke to his right. A dark shape was crouched there and there was a dim red glow. He told himself the lookout, thinking that no one would come to inspect him at this ungodly hour, was having a crafty spit-and-a-draw.

He grinned evilly. Well, if he had his way this was going to be the last smoke the unknown Nip would ever have. Silently he levered his heavy bulk over the rail and crouched there on the deck expectantly. Nothing happened again. The lookout hadn't heard him.

Catlike, McIntyre advanced inch by inch, using any cover the deck provided, sticking, to the shadows, getting ever closer to that dark shadow and the red glow of the cigarette end. Now he could smell the Japanese: that familiar pungent odour of garlic and rotten fish sauces that the Japanese used to flavour their rice. He wrinkled his nose in disgust. In a minute he was going to have to close with the fellow. But he told himself, 'forget the stink and concentrate on nobbling him without a sound.'

He worked his way behind the unsuspecting lookout. Now he was directly behind him. Slowly, very slowly, hardly daring to breathe he reached up one brawny arm. This was the moment of truth. If things went wrong now, there'd be one hell of a battle. He grunted. Next moment he had wrapped his forearm around the lookout's throat.

The man's cigarette fell to the deck. McIntyre tightened his grip and the Japanese wriggled furiously, trying to throw off his assailant. Grimly McIntyre hung on, his face crimson with the effort, the veins at his temples standing out like blood-red worms. 'Come on,' he cursed, 'die, you shit.'

Still the lookout wriggled and fought back. McIntyre slammed his right knee into the small of the other man's back. He gave one last heave. Something snapped. Suddenly, startingly, the lookout went limp in his arm. The Japanese's head lolled to one side.

'*Phew!*' McIntyre breathed out hard. Cautiously, very cautiously, he started to release his hold on the lookout. He didn't move. He was dead all right.

A moment later the big Canadian had dragged the dead lookout into the shadow cast by one of the lifeboats. Then he tiptoed back to the stern. He looked over the side at the white blobs which were faces of the men below. 'Coast clear,' he whispered. 'Let's get cracking. Move it…'

Captain Moto was dreaming. He was seated on a white charger of the kind ridden by his Imperial Majesty, Emperor Hirohito. He was up front at the head of his infantry. The cannons were booming, to left and right shells were falling. They made no impression on his soldiers. They waited in silence, yellow faces stoic and showing no feeling. In their midst fluttered the red and white banner of the rising sun. He felt proud of them and the flag of his beloved Nippon.

He rose in his stirrups, drawing his sword at the same time. The blade glittered a bright silver in the rays of the sun. 'Banzai!'

he yelled.

'*Banzai!*' his soldiers called back, raising their bayonetted rifles into the air.

As one they charged forward. The enemy machine guns began to rattle. Heroically his men continued to charge through the hail of bullets, although soldiers were falling on all sides.

His white charger sprang over the enemy barbed wire. Someone tried to bayonet him, but almost effortlessly he leaned over the side of his mount and lopped off the enemy's head with one blow. Now his men were among the enemy. There weren't many of them left. But they were slashing and stabbing to left and right. Here and there the enemy raised their hands in surrender. But his men had no mercy, only contempt for any soldier who refused to fight to the death. They were bayonetted like the rest. It seemed only a matter of minutes, but then it was all over. The enemy trench was taken, flares started to raise into the sky to signal their triumph to the rest of their division and the flag of Japan fluttered over the trench and the enemy dead. Yet once again, Colonel Moto and his regiment had gained victory for his Imperial Majesty.

Captain Moto woke with a start. He had

been drinking heavily the night before. But his drunken sleep vanished at once. He was totally clear-headed. He had heard a sound, a strange sound. What was it? He listened again. There it was – something striking the hull with a faint muted hollow boom.

He didn't hesitate. He drew on his breeches, put on his glasses and, drawing his samurai sword from his sheath, opened the door of his cabin and went out on to the deck.

By now, a sweating gasping Billy Bennett had manhandled and attached the heavy six-inch shells, three of them, to the gunboat's hull just above the screw. Under CPO Ferguson's direction, the rowing boat had pulled away a little to stern, playing out the explosive cord. Standing in the bows, Smith waited anxiously for McIntyre's return. He knew that the big Canadian had nobbled the lookout, but why wasn't he coming down the anchor chain again? In a minute they would row at least fifty yards from the gunboat to be safe before they could detonate the shells. 'God,' he said to himself, clenching his fists with the tension, 'where the devil is he?'

Next to him CPO Ferguson attached the tape to the detonator box and raised the handle carefully. He patted it to assure himself that the leads were tight and secure. Then turning, he hissed to Smith, 'It's a lash up, sir.'

'Thanks, Chiefie. But hang on a bit. We'll have to wait for Major McIntyre.'

'Ay ay, sir,' CPO Ferguson replied dutifully.

Billy Bennett slumped down besides him with a groan and said, 'Cor ferk a duck, I'm proper knackered, I am.'

'Soft,' Ferguson sneered, 'soft as bluidy putty. You young 'uns dinna ken what real hard work is.'

'Shut up,' Smith snapped irritably.

They 'shut up'. Now all was silent save the faint lap-lap of the water against the gunboat's hull as they waited there, impatient and tense, with the cold wet fog chilling them to the very bone.

Up on deck, McIntyre completed his task. He had decided on the spur of the moment that now he had 'nobbled' the sentry, he might as well put the gunboat's klaxon alarm system out of action. That would stop any quick reaction from the Japanese once the shells had exploded under the stern. With his knife he had cut through the wires which led from the deserted bridge to the sirens. Now he surveyed his handiwork and said to himself in the manner of lonely men, 'That should about do it, I guess.'

He snapped the jacknife closed and was about to put it back in his pocket when he heard the soft pad-pad of naked feet on the deck.

He spun round in sudden alarm. A half-naked figure was coming towards him out of the swirling fog, great curved sword raised above his head. Despite the poor visibility there was no mistaking that portly bespectacled figure. 'Christ Almighty,' McIntyre swore, *'Captain fucking Moto!'*

Chapter Five

Captain Moto drew in his breath sharply. He stamped out his right foot in the ritual manner of a samurai warrior. His left foot followed with that same exaggerated stamp which was designed to put fear into an opponent. Again he drew in his breath very sharply, another part of the ritual.

McIntyre was not in the least afraid. At that moment as the fat little man advanced upon him, stamping his feet and drawing in his breath in this ridiculous fashion, he wondered whether he dare draw his Colt and shoot him. For he didn't know whether the boat crew were finished or not and a shot would cause, he knew, one hell of a flap. Purposefully Captain Moto advanced on the Canadian, stamping and flourishing his sword above his head, muttering fierce oaths and threats in Japanese. He could see that the intruder was transfixed with fear. Obviously he recognized a samurai warrior when he saw one. He was a victim. He could do nothing but accept his fate.

McIntyre's mind raced. The Jap was only ten or so feet away now. In a minute he'd strike. What was he going to do? He pulled out his Colt. Moto saw the gun, it didn't worry him. He was a samurai – nothing could stop him. His sword was all powerful. The little man continued his strange march, puffing mightily, slamming his bare feet to the deck so that it hurt, but he knew no true samurai would surrender to pain. In a moment he would strike mercilessly. He would fell the big intruder with one single blow, cleave his skull in two–

The pistol hit him in the face and caught him completely by surprise. He yelped with pain, stopped in his tracks and lowered his sword momentarily. It was what McIntyre had been hoping for. As the Colt clattered to the deck, he sprang forward. Moto didn't stand a chance against the Canadian's bulk. He slammed to the deck, the sword falling from his grasp. McIntyre clenched his right fist and punched Moto savagely in the face. His spectacles shattered. As did his nose. Blood spurted from it, as McIntyre hit him again.

Suddenly Moto felt overwhelming fear. 'Please don't hit me!' he whimpered in Japanese. McIntyre didn't understand Japanese. It wouldn't have mattered if he had. He was carried away now by a savage Celtic fury. Again his fist ruthlessly slammed into the Japanese's bloody, bruised face. Moto screamed. Hastily McIntyre seized his Colt with his free hand. Now it didn't matter. The scream had alerted the crew and already lights were being clicked on in the officers' cabins. He could hear the sound of running feet, too.

Moto saw the big gun coming close to his feet through the mist of his damaged eyes. 'Don't shoot,' he cried in Japanese, 'please don't shoot!' Even as he pleaded for mercy, he could feel himself evacuating his bowels with fear.

McIntyre showed no mercy. 'Die, you Nip Bastard!' he growled and pressed the trigger. At that range Moto's skull disintegrated like a soft boiled egg struck by a too heavy spoon. Blood and bone flew everywhere in the same instant as flame stabbed the foggy gloom. The big Canadian didn't wait to see who was firing at him. He sprang to his feet, sprinted across the deck and flung himself over the side in a great shallow dive. A moment later he struck the water, went under and next instant was swimming all out for the boat as slugs hit the surface all around him.

Dickie Bird could just hear the distant firing. Straining his ears he could hear the crack of rifle fire and he knew that meant it was the Japanese who were firing because the boarding party had only taken pistols with them. Rifles would have been too cumbersome in such a small boat.

The young officer bit his bottom lip. He had to make a decision. Obviously Smith and his party had run into trouble. How could he help them? Sadie looked at him, her beautiful face worried in the yellow light of the wardroom's single electric bulb. 'Trouble for Mr

Smith?' she said.

'Yes,' he answered laconically.

Dickie Bird thought hard. He knew if he acted as he should, he would endanger the Princess. But could he leave his old shipmates, most of whom he had known since the Great War, in the lurch?

Sadie seemed able to read his mind, for she said, 'Dickie, forget me. Do what you think is best. You are an honourable man. I wouldn't want you to compromise your honour for me.'

He smiled at her. 'That's the first time I have been called an honourable man, especially by a lady,' he replied with a trace of his old flippancy. His smile vanished. In the distance the firing was becoming louder. 'But you're right, Sadie. I couldn't live with myself if I didn't do something now.'

'Then do it,' she said firmly. 'Funny as we Japanese are, we do have a code of honour, the *bushido*. It calls for men – and women, too, I guess – to do the right thing.'

Dickie Bird wasted no further time. 'Close up gun crew!' he commanded before bending down to the voice tube. 'Mac?'

'Ay, ay, sir,' the engineer replied in his thick Glaswegian accent. 'Start her up. We're off.' It wasn't exactly approved Royal Navy procedure, but Dickie Bird was in no mood to observe the niceties of the Admiralty book of rules.

Below his feet the deck began to quiver as the six-inch crew ran to their posts. Suddenly Dickie Bird felt that same sense of fatalistic exhilaration he had back at Kronstadt when they had gone into the Soviet harbour to sink the Red fleet. The sirens had been wailing on the Russian battleship, the *Spartak*. Her pom-poms and heavy machine guns had been hammering away. They had seemed to be riding into a solid wall of glowing lethal tracer. But he had felt no fear, just an exciting thrill of anticipation. If he were going to die, this was the way, young and with his blood hot. Suddenly, to Sadie's astonishment, he yelled, *'Tallyho. We're off. TALLYHO!'*

Sadie said, in not a very genteel manner, 'Oh, my aching arse!'

Slugs were hitting the water all around them. The Japanese were firing from the deck, as the searchlights clicked on. Ginger balancing the Lewis gun the best he could on the gunwhale was firing back, sending tracer zipping across the water in a glowing lethal morse towards the gunboat. The rest of the party was firing too, with CPO

Ferguson yelling in encouragement, 'Come on, laddies, give 'em something to write haim about, ye ken!'

McIntyre rose out of the water. 'Christ,' he panted as he trod water, 'it's like frigging World War II.'

'Thank God,' Smith breathed with relief, thrusting out his hand. 'Get aboard man. We're going to blow the bastard – *now*.' He turned to CPO Ferguson and snapped, 'All right, Chiefie, give the bastard hell, will you!'

'Scotsmen wae hame!' the old petty officer cried gleefully and thrust home the lever of the detonating box.

For one long moment nothing seemed to happen. Then suddenly, there was a slow, soft rumbling. A series of angry red sparks ran the length of the gunboat's stern. The rumbling grew into a roar. It was followed by a deafening explosion. Abruptly the rear end of the Japanese ship rose out of the water. Sailors screamed. Others fell into the suddenly boiling water, arms flailing crazily. For a moment the men in the little boat could see the gunboat's screws as its stern reared into the electric-bright red sky. A second later the gunboat smashed down again, a great hole torn in her stern, sinking swiftly.

'Come on, lads,' Smith cried, 'let's get out of here!'

The men needed no urging. They strained at their oars, as panicked Japanese sailors flung themselves overboard from the sinking craft, while others continued to fire at the men who had so cruelly destroyed their ship. Up in the front of the rowing boat, a soaked McIntyre and Smith snapped off shots to left and right, forcing the Japanese riflemen on the dying ship to keep low. Once a Japanese sailor tried to board their little craft. He didn't have a chance with CPO Ferguson. 'Get off ye fond little yeller bugger!' the old Scot cried and struck him heavily across his shaven skull. The Japanese fell back into the water, dead or unconscious, Ferguson cared not which.

Then slowly they began to draw away from the circle of glowing light, the screams, the curses, the pleas for help, as the stranded vessel sank in the shallow water and the survivors attempted to scramble for safety on the opposite bank. But even as they did so, Smith knew that at daybreak some of the bolder would return to the gunboat to man the gun on the forward deck which was obstinately remaining above the water. Then the little pinnace would have to run the gauntlet of its fire. Why the devil hadn't he ordered Dickie to bring up the craft?

Suddenly his heart gave a great jump of joy. There she was, emerging out of the mist, plodding along at a steady five knots an hour. *The pinnace!* Dickie Bird had made his own decision, the right one. 'Come on, lads,' he yelled joyfully. 'Mr Bird has come to the rescue.'

Five minutes later they were clambering aboard the pinnace, preparing to run by the sunken Japanese gunboat, praying that the gun crew hadn't returned to their stricken craft.

On the bridge, Dickie Bird cried to the engine-room, 'All right, Mac, give her everything you've got.'

The Scot engineer obliged. The Thorneycrofts burst into full power. In a flash, the pinnace, sharp prow high above the water, was surging forward, throwing up a tremendous wake. Dickie Bird knew he was taking a terrible risk in fog like this. But he knew, too, that they had to get by the Japanese gunboat before her crew recovered from the shock of being sunk so surprisingly. Luck was on their side, however.

Apart from a few desultory shots from the bank, the pinnace passed the gunboat safely. Ten minutes later they had slowed down and were plodding steadily down the fog-shrouded Yangtze once more.

'Well,' Smith said with a little sigh, 'that's that.' He wiped the droplets of moisture from the fog off his face wearily. 'Now we're on the last leg of this damned trip. I shall be heartily glad when it's all over. But we've solved the problem of the Nips at least.'

'Not really,' Dickie Bird answered miserably.

Smith looked at his old shipmate in the yellow light of the bridge. 'How do you mean, Dickie?'

'Sadie's a Nip, too, I must remind you, Smithie. What are we going to do about her?'

'You're smitten, old chap, aren't you?'

'Yes, fatally, I'm afraid. Utterly smitten.'

Under other circumstances Smith could have laughed at his friend's woebegone look. How often had Dickie declared that the only kind of women for wandering matelots like they were, were 'the ladies of the night, those fallen beauties, whose charms can be purchased with the coin of the realm.' Now here he was moaning and groaning like some suburban lovesick swain. 'Well, I don't know about that one, Dickie,' he said after a moment. 'It's tricky.'

'Bloody tricky,' Dickie agreed.

Smith yawned and told himself he really was tired. 'All right, Dickie, let's leave it for the time being. I'm going to try to get some shuteye.'

Dickie nodded. 'I'll take over, Smithie.'

Smith went below, leaving Dickie Bird to stare miserably at the fog-shrouded river, telling himself that every mile they went down the Yangtze brought him closer to that overwhelming decision. What *was* he going to do?

Chapter Six

The fisherman sat at the end of the sampan, splitting pumpkin seeds with his rotten teeth and spitting out the coarser bits. Between his bare feet a rough and ready fishing pole rested, the float bobbing up and down in the yellow water of the great river. Behind him on the bank of the Yangtze, there was another similar fisherman, face shrouded by a great straw hat, as if he might be asleep beneath it.

Idly Mr Chen stared at the two fishermen and the teeming life of the bank beyond, where a group of sweat-lathered, half-naked coolies were dragging a chain attached to one of the engineless barges which plied the river. Human beings, he told himself, were cheaper in China than machinery.

'Penny for them, Mr Chen?' McIntyre asked, as he leaned on the rail next to his subordinate, a cheap cigarette clenched between his teeth as usual.

Mr Chen, who understood the English expression, laughed softly. 'My humble thoughts, Major, are not worth even a penny–' He stopped short suddenly and grasped McIntyre's arm. 'Look,' he said urgently.

'Look at what?' McIntyre demanded.

'That man's feet ... and the feet of the other *fisherman*.' Chen pronounced the word as if it were in quotes.

McIntyre stared puzzled in the direction indicated. 'I can't see anything, Mr Chen,' he said after a few moments.

'If they are simple fishermen, why is it they have been wearing boots or shoes?' Mr Chen said with unusual alacrity for him.

'Can't you see the marks made by wearing boots?'

McIntyre whistled softly. 'Yeah, you're right, Mr Chen. I take your point. What are Chinese fishermen doing wearing boots and why have they taken them off to go fishing?'

Mr Chen didn't answer. His mind was racing, trying to find an explanation. Most Chinese peasants went barefoot for nearly all of their lives. At the best they might be able to afford wooden or straw sandals. But boots were definitely out of their reach. He looked once more at the fisherman closest to the passing pinnace. He was a peasant all right. Chen could tell that from the leg muscles. Only peasants used to years of hard work in the paddy fields or on the banks of Yangtze towing motorless barges would have muscles like that. But what kind of peasant would be able to afford boots? Suddenly he had it. 'Major,' he said, 'that fisherman is a soldier.'

'What!'

Mr Chen repeated his statement, adding, 'The only time a peasant gets his hands on boots is when he joins the army. He's a soldier all right.'

'But what kind of a soldier and why is he pretending to be a fisherman?' McIntyre asked in bewilderment, as the fishermen began to drop behind him.

'I can only guess, Major,' Mr Chen answered. 'But that may be some kind of explanation.' He pointed to the bright winking light which had begun to blink off and on up in the low foothills which bordered the great river. 'And I'm sure, he is replying.' He pointed to the second fisherman in the conical straw hat, who had now turned his back on the Yangtze and was facing the hills.

'You mean they're signalling, Mr Chen?'

Mr Chen nodded.

'But why? This is Nationalist territory,' McIntyre objected. 'Why should they be disguising themselves and signalling to some other goddam yo-yo if they're Nationalist soldiers?'

Mr Chen looked at the irate Canadian blandly. 'Because, Major McIntyre, they are not Nationalists.'

'Who in Sam Hill are they then, dammit?'

'Communists.'

'*Communist!*' Smith exclaimed, after McIntyre had finished. 'But what do you make of it? We've seen off the Japs, now the bloody Reds.' He shook his head in bewilderment.

'Remember what C said,' McIntyre explained. 'They've got a stake in starting a war between Nationalist China and Japan. When the balloon goes up they can only profit from it.'

Mr Chen nodded his agreement.

'Oh my sainted aunt!' Dickie Bird breathed. 'Is there no end to this bloody business?'

Mr Chen gave a slight bow. 'This is China, sir,' he said, as if that was explanation enough.

'Too true,' Dickie agreed.

'All right,' Smith cut in briskly. 'What's the drill?'

McIntyre thought for a moment, then he said, 'I think we can expect trouble somewhere between here and Shanghai. I guess we'd better keep our eyes peeled.'

'Right,' Smith agreed. 'From now onwards, we'll keep bashing on regardless. No more stops for food and water. We'll make do with what we've got. There'll be no off-watch crew. We'll all stand lookout till we reach Shanghai,' he flashed a look at Dickie, 'and we deliver the Princess safely to our authorities.' He sighed heartily and added, 'Then gentlemen, I think I never want to see bloody China again. It's too bloody complicated!'

Mr Chen smiled sympathetically. He told himself that it was a sentiment shared in a curiously reversed way by many Chinese of his own type and class. They, too, would be only too happy to see the back of the 'foreign devils' – leave China to the Chinese.

The day passed slowly. By late afternoon it was quite clear that their progress down the Yangtze was being monitored. Signal lamps flashed all the time. More than once they had spotted Chinese peasants watching them through telescopes. At every landing there seemed to be Chinese civilians watching the pinnace sail by, not with the idle curiosity of the average civilian docker or fisherman, but with an intentness that indicated a keen interest in the progress of the British craft. As Dickie Bird put it: 'Those yellow gents are following us, old bean. There's no two ways about it. We're the stars of the show.'

'You're right,' Smith agreed. 'But why? What can they do to us out here, Dickie?'

Dickie shrugged. 'I don't know, old chaps. But I don't think whatever it is it will amount to much good, what.'

'I suppose you're right.' Smith dismissed the matter for time being, saying, 'Well let's keep our eyes peeled, Dickie.'

'Exactly, just like tinned tomatoes, old fruit.' With that he went off on his duties, leaving Smith to stare in puzzled anger at yet another signal lamp blinking off and on in the foothills.

Night fell. Smith decided to weigh anchor in midstream. There was another stretch of narrows ahead and he didn't relish trying to navigate them in the hours of darkness. Most Chinese ships sailed at night without riding lights and the danger of a collision was too great.

Now as on the shores, the villages and hamlets that lined the great river started to light up and the scratch and scrape of Chinese fiddle music began to waft their way. Smith sat in the wardroom with the rest enjoying the first pink gin of the day, while on deck above a double watch paced up and down, watching for intruders. 'We'll each take a spell during the whole night,' Smith said, 'except you Mr Chen. You'll have first watch, Chiefie, then you can get a bit of shuteye afterwards.'

CPO Ferguson, who had been invited into the wardroom for the conference and looked a little embarrassed at being in what he called to his cronies 'officers' country', nodded and said, 'Ay, ay sir. But I'm no that old sir.'

'Come off it, Chiefie,' Dickie Bird chortled, 'we all know you were on the *Victory* the day Nelson was killed.'

Ferguson shot the young officer a dirty look, but said nothing.

'Let's get through this night,' Smith continued, 'and then I think we'll be all right. By evening tomorrow, God willing we shall have reached Shanghai.'

Dickie's grin changed to a frown as he realised what that meant. In Shanghai the Princess, sitting opposite him and looking more beautiful than ever, would have to make her overwhelming decision and he wondered whether he would play any part in it. He looked across at her, but Sadie's dark eyes revealed nothing.

'Each of us,' Smith went on, 'will stay armed and clothed even when he turns in. I want Mac, too, to stand by the engines in case we have to do a sudden bunk.'

'You're taking this very seriously,' McIntyre intoned, drawing on another of his cheap cigarettes. Like the rest of them, he was armed, though this was contrary to King's Regulations. No one was supposed to enter the wardroom armed.

'Yes, I am. Whoever it is who is following is doing so for some purpose or other. What better time to attack than after dark.'

'You're right,' McIntyre agreed. 'OK, I'll take over from CPO Ferguson here, but before I turn in, I want to have another look at the shore. Are you coming Mr Chen?'

Smith yawned mightily. 'Me, I think I'll hit the hay,' he said. 'Good-night everybody.'

So the little group finished off their drinks and broke up, leaving the wardroom to the Princess for that's where Sadie would spend this night; the wardroom was the most secure place on the pinnace. But she too, was armed. Smith and Bird were taking no chances.

On deck, Chen and McIntyre stood in silence, leaning over the rail and staring at the distant shore. There was hardly any traffic on the river now save half a dozen fishing boats, great carbide lanterns glowing a bright incandescent white at their sterns to attract the fish, though McIntyre wouldn't eat a fish from the Yangtze, which acted as a sewer for half of northern China, even if they paid him to.

The blinking lights had ceased, as well, and as far as McIntyre could make out, they were not being observed any longer. 'What do you make of it, Mr Chen? Do you think they've gone away?'

Mr Chen shook his head. 'No, this is the calm before the storm, as you say. My humble person feels it in his bones. There will be trouble this night, Major. I think, if you will allow me to voice an opinion.'

'Fire away.' McIntyre tossed his cigarette end into the water below with a gesture of finality.

'Tonight, we sleep like cat – *with one eye open!*'

McIntyre didn't laugh.

Chapter Seven

Captain K'uang sat on his horse and pondered. Around him, the rest of his cavalry had dismounted and were smoking or chatting a little wearily. It had been a long hard ride following the craft of the foreign devils and they had been forced to loot the last village before the villagers would give them food and drink. That had held them up, too. But now they were in position, though the tall haggard cavalryman and agent was undecided about what to do.

It was obvious that the death squad ordered into action by Borodin was shadowing the pinnace. But how did he contact them and stop their murderous intentions? In the first place he didn't know their leaders or their appearance. They had come straight from the Communist HQ and were unknown to him.

In the end he came to the conclusion that he must wait till they attempted to attack the foreign devils and stop them then. There seemed no other way. Stiffly he got down from his horse, patted its rump and rasped out a few orders, his decision made.

Five minutes later the cavalrymen had settled down for the night, with two outposts closer to the river to observe the silent little craft anchored in the middle of the Yangtze. Captain K'uang clapped his hands in the little tented area he had to himself.

The woman appeared immediately. They had brought her from the village they had looted two hours before. They had found her in the little store next to the merchant's where they sold aphrodisiacs – gingseng, antler fuzz, powdered tiger's teeth and the like which Chinese men thought would bring them more lust in bed. In her case it seemed to work for she was well advanced in pregnancy. As one of the coolies who had watched them loot the two stores had said with a sly grin on his wrinkled toothless face, 'She is very good horse on horse, illustrious one.' And she had come willingly enough.

Now she came in through the opening in the canvas patting her great belly, bare over her silk pants, and making lewd noises.

In spite of his weariness, he laughed softly at her antics, patting herself and chortling like some great mare, swollen with child. 'You make horse-up on-horse,' he said.

'Naturally,' she answered. 'The only way in my condition. Are you ready for it, master?'

He pulled down his cotton trousers and showed her. She gave a fake whistle of admiration. 'You are *very* ready, master.'

'And you?'

By way of an answer, she spread her legs to reveal that her trousers were split in the middle and that she wore nothing underneath. She laughed at the look on his face and said, 'And that's not just for taking a piss. In my business you always have to be ready for – er – action.'

He laughed again. With a grunt, she

straddled him. 'Spear me,' she puffed. 'I'm getting too fat to be nimble.'

He inserted his penis inside her and she gave a contented sigh. 'That feels good, master,' she exclaimed, and lowered her full weight on him. Her huge breasts flew out of the little silk blouse she was wearing, bouncing almost onto his face. 'You suck first,' she urged, giggling, 'then we play horse on horse.'

But Captain K'uang was not fated to play 'horse on horse' this particular night. Suddenly his pleasures were disturbed by the urgent voice of one of his cavalrymen. 'Comrade Captain ... Comrade Captain!'

'Heap of chicken shit,' he cursed and let the woman's nipple drop from his mouth. He gave her a shove and she fell to one side with a loud, wet, sucking noise. She lay there, legs spread wide still, to reveal her sex while he adjusted his pants hastily and stumbled to his feet. 'What is it?' he asked the cavalryman who was panting badly as if he had run all the way from his post on the river bank.

The man swallowed hard. 'Comrade Captain, something strange is going on in the Great Water.'

'What? How strange?' Captain K'uang

rasped angrily.

'I don't know how to explain it, Comrade,' the lookout faltered. 'It's better you come and see for yourself.'

'Oh, all right.' K'uang pulled on his boots while the pregnant woman stared up at him.

'What about me?' she moaned. 'What am I to do with myself?'

Captain K'uang made an obscene suggestion and she laughed with delight, her bare breasts wobbling like jellies. 'I wish I could. But my belly is so big that I can't get my finger round it.'

The two men hastened away, leaving the pregnant woman still squatting, laughing heartily, as if it were all a huge joke.

The moon had risen now, scudding by under the clouds and illuminating the river in its silver spectral light. The captain could see the pinnace, anchored in the middle of the river, a riding light at her bow and stern, quite clearly. Otherwise that stretch of the Yangtze seemed deserted. 'Where is this thing, soldier?' he demanded.

'Over there in the shadows, Comrade Captain,' the man replied. 'It makes strange noises.' He lowered his voice and quavered, 'Do you think it is some kind of water dragon?'

'Don't be a fool, man. Such things don't exist,' Captain K'uang snapped, straining his eyes to penetrate the shadows on the far bank. Suddenly he saw it. It looked like a metal tube, perhaps fifteen metres long, round with something like a mast in its centre and a very long pole projecting from its front; and there was definitely a strange noise coming from it, as the frightened lookout had reported. 'In three devils' name,' K'uang breathed, 'what is it?'

'Magic,' the other man suggested, fear in his voice now. 'Big magic. How can iron float on water? How can iron move when there is no sail ... no motor, answer me that, Comrade Captain?'

'There is no such thing as magic. Magic is like religion, as Karl Marx wrote, the opium of the people.' All the same Captain K'uang was awed and a little frightened, too, by this eerie metal tube which moved forward without any sign of power. How was it worked? What was its purpose?

Abruptly it came to him. He remembered the old sketch and pictures he had seen as a boy when the Japanese had blockaded the Russians at Port Arthur. The sketch had shown how the trapped Russians had tried to break the blockade with a home-made submarine, powered by nine or ten men turning the screw mechanism inside by hand which turned the propeller. To the front of this home-made submarine there had been a long pole to which the defenders had attached a large amount of high explosive. The Russians' intention had been to clamp the high explosive on the side of an enemy ship, back off to a suitable distance and then detonate the explosive with a cable fuse. Unfortunately the Russians had been spotted before they had had time to submerge and Japanese gunners had blown them right out of the water.

Now everything seemed to fall into place. With the one-hundred-percent instant clarity of a vision, Captain K'uang knew these were the killers sent by Nanking to deal with the foreign devils and the Japanese Princess. Somewhere along the Yangtze they had had the crude submarine built and were now about to do what the Russians had attempted – and failed – nearly a quarter of a century before.

The cavalry captain bit his bottom lip. But how could he stop them? His men only had handguns. Their bullets wouldn't penetrate the armoured hide of this home-made sub.

Now the little sub had emerged from the

shadows. In the silver light of the moon, K'uang could clearly see the dark object attached to the end of the long pole sticking out from the bow. Slowly but surely the sub advanced on the unsuspecting pinnace, so low in the water that K'uang felt any lookout the foreign devils might have on the deck of the craft would be unable to see it. The men inside the sub would pack the high explosive against the side of the pinnace and then back off to complete the destruction.

It was just then that he spotted the sub's weak point – the high explosive attached to the pole. Knock that out and the sub would be rendered harmless. He made a quick decision. He turned to the bemused trooper standing next to him, 'Quick, get back to the others. Tell them to come down here at the double with their rifles. Off with you. *Quick!*'

The first volley of rifle fire woke Smith from an uneasy, dream-troubled sleep. He sprang up from his bunk, hand automatically seeking his Colt. Through the tiny porthole he could see the scarlet flashes of fire stabbing the silver darkness. Somebody was firing at them, it appeared from the opposite bank. Hastily, as outside, crew members started to run to their duty stations, he pulled on his boots. He clattered up the steps to the bridge. Dickie was already there. 'What's going on?' he gasped.

'The balloon's gone up. Look–' Dickie pointed to the spurts of fire some two hundred yards away. 'Not very good shots though,' he added.

'Thank God, they aren't.' He pulled the wire. The klaxons started to shriek. On the monkey island Ginger Kerrigan, already seated behind his beloved Lewis guns, yelled above the racket. 'Shall I open fire, sir?'

'Yes, give 'em a burst whoever they are. That might frighten 'em off,' Smith yelled back.

Kerrigan needed no urging. He pressed the trigger. The twin machine guns spurted tracer towards the shore, the glittering line of slugs rising and gathering speed at every instant.

'Bugger your mother! Generation of maggots!' Captain K'uang cursed angrily, as the tracer streamed in their direction. Next to him a soldier yelped with pain and sank to his knees, holding a wounded arm from which the blood spurted in a crimson arc. 'We try to help the ape pizzles and they fire at us. Defiler of dead dogs, suckers of horses' cocks. STOP!'

But the 'defilers of dead dogs, suckers of horses' cocks' didn't stop firing. Unaware of the danger approaching them, now underwater, the crew of the *Swordfish* poured on the fire at the Chinese on the bank. Captain K'uang could have torn his jet-black hair out. What was he to do? Now the crude little submarine could be only a matter of a hundred metres or so from the bow of the unsuspecting foreign devils' craft. Soon the sub would attach the high explosive to its hull. A minute or two later, it would all be over. The foreign devils would die and with them the Japanese Princess. That would mean war between China and Japan, and Borodin had warned him what that would mean for China – and the country, which was the only hope for the masses the world over, the Union of Soviet Russia.

'Bugger my mother-in-law,' the Chinese Captain moaned, as the slugs hit the bank all around him, 'what the *hell* am I to do?'

Chapter Eight

Mr Chen fell to the deck. The impact of the bullet made him gasp with surprise. Next moment he felt the pain, as his legs gave way beneath him. He clutched his hand to his chest, touched something wet and then stared at his palm, red with his own blood, as if he couldn't understand why this was happening to him.

All around him there was noise, the shouts, the hoarse cries, the angry snap-and-crackle of a small arms fight. No one had seen he had been wounded and Mr Chen was a much too modest man to draw attention to himself. 'I shall crawl out of the line of fire,' he told himself. 'Then I shall call for help.' He winced with fresh pain, as a burning sensation swept through his small body. For a moment he thought he was going to black out. There was a loud ringing noise in his ears. Automatically he shook his head. Next moment he wished he hadn't. Blood started to spurt in a bright red arc from the wound in his chest.

He bit his bottom lip and began to crawl. He muttered to himself as he did so, a mixture of curses and pleas for help. But no help came. The crew of the pinnace were too occupied with their supposed attackers.

Suddenly Mr Chen stopped short. In the silver light of the moon, he could see something moving very slowly towards the pinnace. He blinked his eyes, for they were refusing to focus correctly. The object came into view once more. It looked like a large log. But what was the bundle attached to some sort of cable at its tip?

Mr Chen pondered, for what seemed to him in his ever weakening state, a long time. On the deck below him, the planks were wet with his blood. But he didn't notice. He appeared fascinated by the log and the bundle, which were some thirty metres away. What were they?

Abruptly he had it. The log was to be rammed into the side of the pinnace. The bundle was high explosive. In that same moment he could hear the faint creakings of some sort of metallic device and he could see the shadowy outline just below the surface of the river.

Weak as he was, Mr Chen knew he had to do something. If he didn't, not only he but the men he called privately 'foreign devils' would die. He knew that instinctively. Foreign devils they certainly were, but they were his friends, too. Major McIntyre, Smith, Dickie Bird and all the rest of them. *He had to do something!*

Slowly, awfully slowly, his hand, wet with his own blood, slid to his pocket where he had his pistol. Somehow or other he got it out. Now the underwater object was only twenty metres away. He could hear the faint noise it made quite clearly. He clicked off the 'safety'. He raised the pistol. His hand trembled violently and a black mist kept descending over his eyes. He blinked and fought it off.

'Come,' he muttered crazily to himself and aimed the pistol. The sight crossed the edge of the log. He knew he couldn't hold the pistol up much longer – it weighed so heavily. It took all his remaining strength to do so, then he pressed the trigger.

There was an enormous explosion. Angry red light split the silver gloom. The blast like a blow from a flabby fist struck Mr Chen in the face. He blinked his eyes once more as the debris started to rain down into the water. The object had gone. He had destroyed it. A faint smile crossed his pain-contorted face for an instant then Mr Chen fell to one side unconscious...

'He's dying, I'm afraid,' McIntyre said, rising to his feet. 'He's bleeding internally. I've seen it before in the last show.' The big Canadian pointed to the blood on the black leather wardroom couch where they had placed him. 'He's bleeding from the rectum. That blast must have torn his guts to pieces.'

Sadie looked in horror at the dying Chinaman, eyes full of tears. 'Is there nothing we can do?'

McIntyre shook his head sadly and now there were tears in his eyes too. 'Poor old bugger,' he said huskily. 'If we were in Shanghai, there might be some quack who could help him. But we're not.'

Sadie turned her head away so that the others couldn't see she was weeping, while on the couch Mr Chen's eyes flickered open. 'Shanghai,' he repeated the name weakly, while they strained to hear his words. 'In Shanghai if ... a white man ran over a Chinese, he paid four hundred dollars ... and the whole matter was forgotten... Chinese are not of value there.' Mr Chen gave a queer kind of laugh. 'No dogs or Chinks, they say in the International Settlement...'

Staring at him Smith could see the end of his nose becoming white and pinched. He knew what that meant. Mr Chen was dying. He had seen enough men at the edge of death look like that.

'They took our lands from us – Shanghai, Hong Kong ... the rest... Now we must have them back... China for the Chinks.' He gave a deep throaty cough, which seemed to tear his whole body apart. Blood seeped from the edge of his mouth. Abruptly with a note of absolute finality, his head lolled to one side. He was dead.

McIntyre stared at him. Slowly, very slowly, he put out his big hand, fingers extended and closed Mr Chen's eyes. 'Don't know whether Chinks, do that. But I'm doing it for him,' he said, voice hoarse. 'Good Chink ... Mr Chen was.' He walked over to the cabinet, poured himself a glass of pink gin and downed it in one go.

It was dawn. The Yangtze was crowded with junks, sampans, a few tramp steamers, the usual traffic of the great river heading for Shanghai.

CPO Ferguson had sewn up Mr Chen in the traditional canvas. Now only his face was visible. CPO Ferguson grunted and then carried out the traditional last rite. He poked his needle through Mr Chen's lower lip. It was a custom dating back to Nelson's time, a means of ascertaining whether a sailor was really dead before they buried him at sea.

Dickie Bird winced, as CPO Ferguson now turned his attention to sewing up the canvas over the face, saying, 'Ay, yon wee feller was nae bad for a Chink.'

Ginger Kerrigan and Billy Bennett waited till the CPO was finished, then draped the Union Jack – McIntyre had insisted strongly on that – over the canvas-shrouded dead body. They bent in unison and picked him up, the canvas already stained at the back with his blood. At the rail, another two sailors braced the board over which the dead men would slide, ready for the shroud.

Awkwardly Smith cleared his throat and said, 'Shipmates, I don't know what religion Mr Chen was. All I know, he acted as a Christian gentleman should. He saved our ship and perhaps our lives.' He paused and noted that Sadie was crying again. 'So I'll commend him to the deep and his Maker with the gratitude of everyone here, I know.'

There was a murmur of 'here, here', and McIntyre dabbed the corner of his eye.

CPO Ferguson felt the foot of the canvas

shroud to check whether the leaded weights were there. They were. He nodded to Kerrigan and Bennett. They let go of the shroud. Noiselessly the shroud containing the body slid down the plank. It hit the water with a splash and went under immediately.

For a few moments the silent crew stared at the spot and then, as if in response to some unspoken command, they drifted away to their duties, no one speaking as they did so.

An instant later Smith broke the heavy silence, saying, 'In about an hour we'll be seeing the Shanghai Bund, gentlemen. Then something will have to be decided about what to do with Sadie.' He looked earnestly at Dickie Bird.

'You must understand,' he added, looking at McIntyre now, 'that her life will be still in danger in Shanghai. And we are known for who we are and she, too. The less time we spend in that place the better.'

Dickie Bird remained silent, too concerned with his own problems to speak, but McIntyre saw immediately what Smith meant.

'Can't we take the pinnace,' he said, 'and go down the coast to Hong Kong with her?

From there we'd be able to go to some safe place.'

Smith shook his head. 'We're marked through the pinnace as it is and I doubt if the Rear Admiral Yangtze would approve of losing the pinnace. After all it is his newest craft and he'd never be able to get a replacement. Their Lordships back in Whitehall are cutting costs all the time. No.' He shook his head firmly.

For a while there was silence while the other two considered his words, each man wrapped in a cocoon of his own private thoughts. Now ahead they could see the haze that hung over Shanghai, a compound of the smoke coming from its many textile factories and sweatshops and the fumes of the port's car-crowded streets. In the far distance they could see the dark dot circling over the area. Smith strained his eyes and said, 'Look, one of those newfangled flying boats.'

McIntyre looked in the direction indicated and slowly, very slowly, his craggy face started to crack into a tough grin. 'Hot damn,' he cried suddenly, startling the other two, 'I've got it!'

'What?' the other two asked in unison.

McIntyre answered their question with

another one. 'Do you know whose flying boat that is?' he asked.

Smith shrugged and Dickie Bird shook his head, saying, 'Search me, old bean.'

'Well, I'll tell you. It belongs to General Tanaka.'

'You mean the Jap premier?' Smith said.

'Yep. We – me and Mr Chen – were interested in it because we found out it flew the regular secure courier service between Tanaka and his stooge General Kameyama in the International Settlement. That's how the Nip got his orders.'

'So?' Smith asked puzzled, as the seaplane disappeared over the horizon.

'So, 'McIntyre echoed, his grin getting even broader, as he added more detail to his new scheme. 'I now know how to get Sadie out of Shanghai toot sweet.'

Chapter Nine

They had hired the little boat just off the Nanking Road. Now with the great city settling down for the night, they rowed with muffled oars towards the silent flying boat.

Two or three hours before, coins had changed hands and their informant, one of the hundreds of petty spies who peopled Shanghai, had told Major McIntyre all he needed to know about the Japanese seaplane.

All the crew, including the pilot, slept aboard the craft – the Japanese were always pathologically afraid of sabotage – and were due to take off back to Tokyo at dawn. McIntyre knew, too, that the nearest Japanese gunboat was over a mile away at the other end of the Bund embankment. Their task then would be basically to overpower the flying boat's crew.

'Of course,' Smith had objected mildly when McIntyre had explained his bold plan, 'you're breaking every rule in the book. In peacetime you don't do that kind of thing.'

McIntyre had shot him a look that said, 'grow up, brother', and had snapped, 'What do you think those Nips under Captain Moto were doing all the time up the Yangtze – *playing croquet!* Nah, the Nips are fighting an undeclared war already.' McIntyre's face had hardened even more. 'They don't play by the rules, why the hell should we?'

Now he, Smith and Bird, supported by Ginger Kerrigan and Billy Bennett, steered the little sampan out of the great fleet of similar craft towards the flying boat. To all intents and purposes, they could be just another Chinese fishing sampan heading out to the China Sea for a day's fishing for those fat prawns which the richer Chinese loved. Behind them the city was growing ever more silent. Now only occasionally could they hear the irate honking of a horn from the great stone chasm of the Bund. By now even the clubs, the hub of the International Settlement's social life, would have closed.

'There are two doors in the hull,' McIntyre informed them, as they came ever closer to their objective, 'one right up front on the hull for the use of the pilot and crew. The other one, for the use of passengers, in the middle of the hull. I think the crew will probably sleep in the back cabin. So I suggest we go in through the front door.'

'If it's open,' Dickie Bird interjected.

'It'd better be,' McIntyre said grimly. 'Otherwise there–' He didn't finish the sentence, but the others knew what he meant. There would be a fight and that might mean damage to the plane, something which they couldn't afford.

They sailed on slowly. Now they could see

the outline of the flying boat quite clearly. It was tied up to a large buoy and it moved gently with the sway of the water. Otherwise nothing stirred. It was obvious the Japanese crew suspected nothing. McIntyre nodded his head, as if in approval.

'Motorboat coming,' Smith hissed urgently. 'To starboard.'

The other two swung round startled. A motorboat was coming towards them at speed. McIntyre recognized it immediately. 'International police patrol,' he snapped.

'What's that?' Smith asked.

'They protect the International Settlement. See there are no dead Chinks on the Bund in the morning and check that international craft are okay at night. Look.'

A searchlight had clicked on suddenly. Its harsh white beam swept the water near the flying boat and then ran the length of the plane itself.

'*Duck!*' McIntyre hissed urgently. 'The light's coming our way.'

As one they did so. The light hit the little sampan, as the motorboat stopped moving. It was as if the International Police Patrol suspected that something was wrong about this sampan so close to the Japanese flying boat. They tensed, hardly daring to breathe.

The light seemed to bear down upon them for an eternity.

Then it moved on. Dickie Bird breathed a sigh of relief and was about to raise his head, when McIntyre snapped warningly, 'Not yet!'

Bird ducked in the very same instant that the beam of the searchlight swung back onto the sampan once more. This time, however, it hovered there for only a fraction of a second before it went off altogether. Moments later someone opened the motor boat's throttle and it roared away into night, throwing up a huge wake.

'That nearly tore it,' Dickie Bird said.

'An old trick,' McIntyre said. 'Used it myself. Now come on. Let's get to that Nip plane. That goddam motorboat engine will have awakened the frigging dead.'

Five minutes later they nudged up to the buoy to which the flying boat was tethered. McIntyre went to work immediately, as they had planned. With his knife he sawed through the cable, while the other two held on.

In seconds it was completed. Now the flying boat was in their hands. 'All right,' Dickie Bird said, 'I've got it.' He gritted his teeth as he took the strain. 'Get moving.'

They needed no urging. They knew they had to get away from this spot just in case the International Police Patrol boat returned. Both Smith and McIntyre joined the two ratings at the great oars, taking the enormous strain, while Dickie Bird stared anxiously at the bulk of the flying boat waiting for the first sign that the crew noted that something was amiss.

Slowly, very slowly, the flying boat began to move. Smith's muscles felt as if someone were poking them with a red-hot iron. Still he and the rest persevered. They knew they had to get the Japanese craft out of the central harbour before they dared set about the dangerous task of trying to break into it. So they strained and panted, hauling the heavy flying boat after them, praying as they did so that the police boat wouldn't turn up once more.

Time passed in back-breaking work. Inspite of the night chill, all of them were lathered with sweat and Dickie Bird holding on to the flying boat felt his arms would soon be dragged out of their sockets under the immense strain. Grimly he bit his bottom lip till the blood flowed.

Now they were almost at the rendezvous agreed upon with the CPO Ferguson. Smith ordered the men to stop rowing and they slumped gratefully over their oars, panting hard, but with their eyes fixed on the Japanese flying boat. Still it remained silent. None of the crew had noticed that the craft had been taken from its moorings.

Smith took the signalling lamp from the bottom of the sampan. He flicked it off and on three times, the agreed signal.

Some way off came back the answering signal, followed a few moments later by the sound of engines starting up. CPO Ferguson had seen them and was on his way.

McIntyre said, 'We go in as soon as Ferguson arrives.' He looked grim and determined in the moonlight. 'Use your fists and coshes. We use firearms at the last resort. Above all the pilot must be unharmed. We need him. Clear?'

They nodded their understanding.

Now the sound of powerful engines grew ever closer. They stared hard at the flying boat to check whether the noise had woken the crew yet. Apparently it hadn't. The flying boat remained silent, with not a light showing.

A few minutes later the pinnace hove to, cutting through the water, engines stopped, for the last hundred yards or so to where the sampan floated. There was a quick whispered exchange between the two craft and then McIntyre said, rising to his feet, 'Here we go.'

On the rail of the pinnace, Sadie hissed, 'Oh, do be careful, all of you, please.'

McIntyre reached up and caught hold of the nearest strut. He pulled himself up by it and reached for the handle of the door which led to the pilot's compartment. Gingerly he started to turn it while the others stared up at him tensely. It seemed to take an age before he turned and whispered softly, 'It's unlocked. I'm going in. Follow me.'

He opened the metal door and went in. Immediately Dickie Bird, carrying a cosh made of a woollen sock filled with earth, clambered up after him.

Cautiously the two of them, as Ginger and Billy Bennett followed, threaded their way through the pilots' seat, trying to avoid bumping into anything in the gloom. Now they could hear the snores coming inside the plane. McIntyre hesitated at the door which separated the two compartments. He drew his pistol.

He looked back at the others crowded together in the cockpit. They nodded.

'OK, here we go!' With a grunt he wrenched the door open, pistol at the ready in his other hand.

Four Japanese were curled up in the seats of the outer cabin, huddled in blankets. McIntyre didn't hesitate. He turned on the light switch and said, 'Hands up ... come on ... *hands up!*'

The four small men, clad in singlets and droopy underpants, rose from their makeshift beds, startled. One of them started to cry out, but he stopped short when he saw the white men crowded in the doorway, all of them armed.

'Come on,' McIntyre repeated threateningly, 'get those hands up. Hurry up!' He jerked up the muzzle of his pistol to emphasize his meaning.

Reluctantly they did so, with one of them, a burly man with the look of a fighter about him, saying, 'What you do? This not legal.' He pronounced the word as 'regal'.

'Just do as you're told,' McIntyre answered. 'Now all of you on to your feet. Move it.'

Confused and angry, the four men did as they were commanded, and McIntyre asked, 'Who is the pilot among you?'

It was the burly little man with the

fighter's face. 'I am pilot,' he answered with a surly look, but his eyes were quick with life. Suddenly he raised his voice and shouted something in Japanese. The curtain which McIntyre had thought hid the plane's lavatory was thrown back abruptly to reveal a proper bed there and a small, elderly man, with a pistol in his hand.

'Christ Almighty,' McIntyre yelled, as the old man fired, 'it's General Kameyama!'

Behind McIntyre, Ginger Kerrigan yelped with pain, as the bullet slammed into his shoulder. He staggered and would have fallen if Billy Bennett hadn't caught him in time.

Rage surged through McIntyre's body. He thought of the dead Mr Chen, who had died because of Kameyama. 'You old bastard,' he cried, as the Japanese between ducked for cover and the General prepared to fire again, 'try this one on for size.' He pressed his trigger.

The big Colt spat fire. The slug hit the General in the belly. At such close range, the impact lifted Kameyama right off his feet. He flew backwards and smacked into the rumpled bed which he had just vacated.

The Japanese pilot made as if he were going to run and help the old General who was moaning and writhing on the bed in pain, as the intestines poured from his torn open stomach like a great steaming grey-red snake.

'Hold it,' McIntyre snarled, face still furious with rage. 'Let the old bugger die in pain. He deserves it.'

'But he is general,' the pilot objected.

'He's fucking nothing,' McIntyre rasped. 'He's soon going to be a dead man. Now up here. *Quick!*'

Smith turned to Ginger as the pilot came forward reluctantly. 'You're going with them, Ginger. Hong Kong's only an hour away by air. They'll patch you up all right there.'

'Ain't been in an hairy plane,' Ginger tried to joke weakly, while a worried Billy Bennett supported him.

'You, too, to give Ginger here a hand,' Smith snapped, 'and to keep an eye on the Nips. That'll mean, three of you, McIntyre included, and the Princess.'

Dickie Bird looked unhappy. Smith knew why, but there was nothing he could do about that. He ignored his old shipmate's miserable look. For people like them and, indeed, the whole crew of the old *Swordfish* there could be no conventional happy family life. They were part of the 'great game' as C always called it, secret warriors who were doomed to fight a war in the shadows to which there was only one outcome – *death*.

On the bloodstained bed, the old general was still alive, moaning softly, but conscious. As he saw Sadie enter the plane, he raised himself with one last effort and pointed a trembling finger at her. He mumbled something in Japanese and she faltered so much that Dickie Bird caught her arm in alarm, in case she fell over. 'What did he say?' he asked the white-faced Princess.

She hesitated, 'He said I am a traitor ... and ... a whore.'

'The rotten swine,' Dickie exploded. 'If he weren't already dying, I'd punch his bloody nose for him.'

The old man, his wrinkled face contorted with hate, his eyes venomous, said something else. Then with a soft groan he fell back on the bloodstained bed. General Kameyama was dead.

'What did he say now?' Dickie asked.

She hesitated, her face even more shocked. 'That there is no escape for me. I have betrayed my class and people. There is nowhere that I can run.' She looked at him, eyes brimming with tears. 'He's right, Dickie.'

'But Sadie–'

She put her finger to his lips softly to stop him. 'I will always think of you,' she said.

Ten minutes later the flying boat was ready to depart, with Billy Bennett and McIntyre watching the four man crew suspiciously.

They caught a last glimpse of her beautiful sad face through the porthole and then the plane began to move away, gathering speed by the instant, setting off on its flight to Hong Kong, where Sadie would somehow disappear.

Smith and Dickie Bird watched the flying boat beginning to rise, the sound of its engines getting softer by the second and then it was gone, vanished into the darkness.

For what seemed a long while the two old friends, who had known each other since school, stared after it in total silence. Then Smith broke the silence, with, 'Come along, Dickie old pal. Rear Admiral Tangze is smuggling us out of Shanghai at dawn with one of his insects – *HMS Wasp*. She's going back to Bombay for a refit.'

Dickie Bird shook his head, as if awaking from a deep sleep with difficulty. 'I see,' he said.

Together they walked to the opposite rail of the pinnace and stared at the stark towering skyline of Shanghai's Bund. 'In three hours time,' Smith said slowly, 'we'll be seeing the last of that – and China. I, for one, will be glad.' He shook his head.

'Yes, the things we've seen and done since we arrived here,' Dickie Bird agreed softly.

'As I said at the beginning, gentlemen,' CPO Ferguson butted in, 'yon Chinks are a heathen lot. Always have been, always will be. They'll never change, mark my words, gentlemen.' Grimly he spat over the side into the dirty brown water. 'Guid night t'ye, gentlemen.' He turned and disappeared into the gloom from which he had come.

Smith forced a smile. 'Well, Dickie, that's as good an epitaph on China as any. Come on, let's go over to the wardroom, have a pink gin and get our heads down till dawn.' He thrust his arm through that of his friend and they turned to disappear into the gloom as well.

ENVOI

Days Of Wine And Roses

Rear Admiral Sir William Bird, D.S.O, D.S.C, stepped from the trim launch and stared up at the huge bulk of the *US Missouri*, the biggest ship afloat in the world, he knew. With his one good arm, he grasped the highly polished starboard ladder and started to climb the steep ascent to the deck where the historic ceremony was to be held.

A US marine sentry saluted him and an officer of the deck, dressed in starched khakis, seeing his one arm said, 'Can I help you, Admiral?'

'No thank you, Ensign,' Sir William said. 'Please tell me where the surrender ceremony is to be held.'

The officer of the deck told him and when the Admiral had strode away in the direction indicated, he muttered under his breath to the marine sentry, 'Jesus H. Christ, who's that guy? One arm and one eye with a black patch – Nelson?'

'Don't know, sir,' the sentry replied woodenly. 'Never heard of that guy, Nelson. Some kinda limey?'

The brass was assembled on the quarterdeck. Most were Americans, but there were Britons, too, Dutch in quaint caps, Russians in red-striped trousers and half a dozen other Allied nations, all present this September day in Tokyo Bay to celebrate their defeat of the last enemy, Imperial Japan. Now they had formed up in a U around an old mess table, covered with green baize, with chairs on both sides of it. Here General Douglas MacArthur, the Allied Supreme Commander, would accept the surrender by the Japanese delegation.

Quietly Sir William Bird took his place directly behind General Percival, buck-teethed and emaciated from three years in a Japanese prison camp. He was the man who had surrendered Singapore to the enemy back in 1942. Next to him was American General Wainwright, equally skinny and grey-skinned, who had been the last defender of the Philippines before he, too, had surrendered to the Japanese.

Sir William sighed a little helplessly. It had been a long war and he was tired. He had lost an eye at Crete and an arm on D-Day. Now he would dearly have loved to have gone home and rested. But he no longer had a home or a family to go home to. Both had been destroyed and killed during the great blitz on Plymouth back in 1940. He was alone in the world. All he had left was the Royal Navy and his ship.

'Attention all hands!' came a sharp command from an American officer. Obediently the top brass clicked to attention as if they were young officers again. It was the Japanese surrender delegation coming aboard.

Some officers smiled at the sight. Others bristled like dogs at their hated enemies. Here and there faces were set in contemptuous sneer. The Japanese Imperialists, who had spread so much terror throughout the Far East, were being humiliated at last. The Nation which never surrendered was now surrendering.

The Japanese diplomats wore top hats and cutaways. The Japanese generals were hung with gold braid, chests splendid with row after row of medal ribbons. An American officer indicated where they should stand in four ranks to await the Allied Supreme Commander. They halted, yellow faces sullen and set.

Five minutes passed. MacArthur was making the Japanese wait deliberately, Sir William Bird told himself. He was rubbing their noses in salt, rightly so. For a moment he recalled how arrogant the Japs had been when he had been a young man on the Yangtze, little bespectacled men swaggering around with those absurdly long samurai swords of theirs.

'Here he comes,' the red-tabbed British general next to him whispered out of the side of his mouth, 'MacArthur.'

Flanked by two admirals of the fleet who now peeled off to left and right, America's most famous soldier came striding towards the table. He was dressed simply in a khaki shirt and slacks, with not a single medal ribbon on his broad chest, in contrast to all the other officers present there.

MacArthur halted. The Japanese bowed low. He didn't salute in return. Instead he took a single sheet of paper out of his pocket, his big hand marked with liver spots, trembling slightly. He started to read what was written on the paper immediately, as a diminutive woman in the uniform of the American WACs prepared to translate his words into Japanese.

'We are gathered here, representatives of the major warring powers to conclude a solemn agreement whereby peace may be restored... It is my earnest hope that a better world will emerge...'

Suddenly MacArthur's words were forgotten as Sir William stared hard at the middle-aged Japanese-American woman translating them. 'Could it be?' he half-whispered to himself.

'What's that?' his neighbour, the red-tabbed General, asked.

'Sorry ... nothing,' he answered embarrassed.

He stared hard at the interpreter, as MacArthur said, 'As Supreme Commander for the Allied Powers, I announce it is my firm purpose ... to insure that the terms of surrender are fully, promptly and faithfully complied with...'

The face was older and the figure a little fuller, but surely it was her. There was no mistaking that melodious voice even though she was speaking Japanese. It *had* to be her.

Now the cameras clacked and whirred as the Japanese started to sign the two instruments of capitulation, one bound in leather for the Allies, the other canvas-bound for the Japanese.

One by one they stepped forward to add their signature to the document which would end World War Two. Face impassive, MacArthur waited until they were finished, then he spoke into the microphone for a broadcast to the American people, determined to have the first words of peace. 'Today the guns are silent,' he said, while the WAC Major stepped back and stared at the beaten Japanese. 'A great tragedy has ended. A great victory has been won... The entire world is at peace. The holy mission has been completed.'

Sir William felt his heart leap as he watched the tears trickle down the interpreter's face as she listened. It was her. *It was Sadie!*

'Now we have had our last chance. If we do not now devise some greater and more equitable system, Armageddon will be at our door,' MacArthur was saying in that fine vibrant voice of his. 'And today my fellow countrymen, I report to you that your sons and daughters have served you well... They are homeward bound – take care of them!'

The surrender ceremony was over. The top brass broke up to go the Fleet Commander's wardroom for coffee and doughnuts. But Sir William Bird didn't follow them. American ships were 'dry' and at this moment he would dearly have loved a stiff drink, a double pink gin like he and Smithie had used to down in the old days when they were young.

Slowly, almost hesitantly, for a man who

had been in the thick of the war on every sea front since 1939, he walked to where the American lady major stood, staring at Tokyo in the distance, wrapped up in a cocoon of her own thoughts. She didn't hear him coming. He stopped and cleared his throat. He didn't want to startle her, he told himself. Or was it apprehension?

She turned and looked at him. Her face was as beautiful as ever. 'Admiral?' she said puzzled.

'Princess ... Sadie,' he stuttered, feeling suddenly as naive and as embarrassed as he had been that day so long before when he had first met her.

Her eyes remained puzzled. 'I don't understand,' she said slowly. 'No one has called me Sadie for a long time. Did I know you once, perhaps?'

Tears shot to his one eye. He pulled himself together, just like that day off Crete when the survivors of the sunken destroyer had been floating on a piece of wreckage and the surgeon commander had said in a very matter-of-fact way, 'Dickie, old chap, I think I'm going to have to take that eye of yours out if you're going to live.' His thoughts returned to the present. 'Yes, you did,' he said simply.

Suddenly her eyes lit up as she recognized him. 'You're Dickie!' she blurted out excitedly. 'Dickie ... Bird!'

His confusion vanished. 'Yes, silly young Dickie Bird, though no one ever dare call me Dickie these days.'

Her eyes fell on his chest with the row after row of medal ribbons and the heavy gold braid of his white naval cap. 'No, I don't suppose they would,' she said. 'You've been to the wars,' she added a little lamely.

'Yes, the poor man's Nelson, I'm afraid,' he said. He spotted the ring on her finger. 'Married?'

'*Was*. Husband killed with the 422nd Nisei Regiment – you know Japanese-American, in France last year. You?'

His smile vanished. 'Killed in the blitz five years ago.'

'So many people killed. Your guys?'

'Think Smith – old Common Smith's alive – but all the rest are long gone. The war, you know,' he said, as if that explained everything.

'The war.' Suddenly she reached out her hand and took his. It was the first time a woman had touched him in five years. 'Dickie,' she said and then her voice broke.

So it was that the crew of the *USS Missouri*

were treated to the spectacle of a British admiral walking hand-in-hand with a Japanese major in the US Army...

The publishers hope that this book has given you enjoyable reading. Large Print Books are especially designed to be as easy to see and hold as possible. If you wish a complete list of our books please ask at your local library or write directly to:

Magna Large Print Books
Magna House, Long Preston,
Skipton, North Yorkshire.
BD23 4ND

This Large Print Book, for people who cannot read normal print, is published under the auspices of

THE ULVERSCROFT FOUNDATION

… we hope you have enjoyed this book. Please think for a moment about those who have worse eyesight than you … and are unable to even read or enjoy Large Print without great difficulty.

You can help them by sending a donation, large or small, to:

The Ulverscroft Foundation, 1, The Green, Bradgate Road, Anstey, Leicestershire, LE7 7FU, England.
or request a copy of our brochure for more details.

The Foundation will use all donations to assist those people who are visually impaired and need special attention with medical research, diagnosis and treatment.

Thank you very much for your help.